A Bot under

Gödel's Curse

Klaus Wimmer

mcre publishing

MCRE Verlag
www.mcreverlag.de

ISBN-13   978-3943310085
Cover images Daniel Schneider

For Nancy Elaine
and Stephanie Ann

Many thanks, my friends.

Foreword

I write of people I met, places I know, episodes I witnessed, and of ideas which fascinated me.

The names of all players are made up.

Klaus Wimmer

1

The Institute

Cybermafia

Bold Ideas

Vicious Cycle

Eugen waited in the quiet east of the Aleksandrovsky Park, apart from the restaurants, playgrounds and promenades in the west. On this bench he would meet Pjotr. He scanned the silhouette of roofs across the park, the monumental flat roofs constructed under the tsars, then the cubes and turrets of soviet builders. Way down, lit by the June sun, he recognized a gable, the roof of the institute.

Eugen loved the French charm of this old building, once home of the Huguenot family du Mesnil. Portraits still decorated the staircase – memories of the pioneers called in by Tsar Peter the Great to drain the swamps on which St. Petersburg was to grow. Portraits of craftsmen followed who built the harbor and ships, along with all the other immigrants of the Russian Empire. All residents of this house won outstanding merits, the Mesnils as well as the scientists of the highly awarded institute later on.

Eugen had not thought of his institute in a long time. It vanished after the collapse of the Soviet Union like so many other things. He did not grieve. Amused he watched the tussling crows before him and did not notice a limousine stopping at the curb. A chauffeur opened the door, an elegantly clad man stepped out and approached him.

When Pjotr sat down on the bench next to him, both men exchanged merely a glance. Eugen did not recognize the tailor-made suit, nor the Patek Philippe watch or the Gucci shoes. Pjotr, however, observed Eugen's scraggy hair, the ragged jacket and the worn out, once-elegant shoes.

Pjotr knew, all the brainiacs in Eugen's team had instantly found new jobs after the demise of the USSR. China, India, Pakistan, Iran and Israel had raised their military budgets and the run for Russian specialists was on.

Only Eugen remained – the best of them all. Did he have issues, alcohol or drugs perhaps, ailments or madness?

Pjotr had shadowed him and learned that Eugen had not accepted an offer of the University of Kiev, but had stayed in his humble apartment.

Eugen had delayed this meeting repeatedly. Months ago, Pjotr had urged him to come along to the Carnival in Rio: he had to allow himself the Samba girls at least once in his life. Then Pjotr invited him to spend spring in Cyprus, this corner of paradise where friendly Middle Easteners coddled rich Russians.

Eugen may have given in to Pjotr's wooing. They knew each other well since their days at Lyceum 241, a training ground for the Communiast Party's high potentials. But obviously Pjotr wanted to use him for shady business.

Pjotr: „Still watching crows? You haven't changed."

„They fascinate me, as always."

„Raven rabble, boring beasts."

„Look closer, how elegant they are; strong, playful and clever."

„I remember, you called your robot *Sea Crow*, SC 13."

„Then you know why."

„13?"

„Well, twelve foundered, Version 13 marked the break-through at last. Version 5 still lies back there in the harbor. We never found it."

Eugen had broken into Pjotr's computers and snooped around. Pjotr seemed to run a cyber-crime-business, earning splendidly by hacking and blackmailing financial institutions around the globe. Banks pay up swiftly to retain their trusting clientele. *Dreary business. Nauseating,* Eugen thought, *leeched technology in the hands of a man without perspective.*

What on earth did this crook want of him? Why lure him with a few measly dollars, why not hire those hungry hackers hanging around by the dozens?

But Pjotr had plans. He wanted to expand his craft and move to where the gold-mines lay: business with cyber-terror. Thus, in future he needed more than his bread & butter tricks, more than breaking computer firewalls.

His new customers would demand the disruption or destruction of complex systems like airports or power plants. Terror paid off if it could threaten to paralyze gas-pipelines, oil terminals or the IT-infrastructure of the capital-market. The main nodes of the Internet were still untouchable. But Pjotr was certain, this jackpot, too, was in reach.

His future business meant cooperation with the biggies: foreign secret services, international terror organizations, arms and drug syndicates. He would provide special services for the specialized demands of well-heeled clients.

Pjotr was aware of his only choice: to get richy or, be dispatched and thrown to the wolves. He would have to depend on the excellence of his crew more than ever. Hence he had come.

Eugen had the intellectual acumen to revolutionize the cyber-future. Trojans, worms, viruses and all the other tools in his toolbox had been invented around 1970 and their evolution was now coming to an end. Cyber-attacks called for a technical quantum leap and Eugen could achieve it.

Pjotr: „My friend, you know what's up. Want to give it a shot?"

When Eugen shook his head, Pjotr produced a wad of $1000 bills and thumbed it through.

„Half a million now. More later."

Eugen did not react.

„No? Perhaps you prefer diamonds?"

He pulled a cedar wood box from his pocket, showed its exquisite intarsia and opened the lid. Crystals sparkled in the sunlight. He handed the box to Eugen, who shook his head again.

„That's a damned heap of money for a piece of software", Pjotr said.

Now Eugen turned to Pjotr:

„Piece of software? You are missing the boat. Listen. I'll give you the low down.

Today, I played Bach's Brandenburg Concertos – the world's most beautiful music. Tey are grand masterpieces, unsurpassed for 300 years, delighting millions of people.

Don't even guess what its mark-to-market is. It is invaluable. Now remember this: my theory will match this music. Can you grasp that?"

Pjotr turned to Eugen:

"Your stuff is way over my head. But I do understand what you like best: playing your own game. What a shame. We would have been a great team. The best in the market."

The meeting was over. Pjotr went back to his car, leaving Eugen in the light of the evening. Again Eugen watched the crows, the elegant curve from the tip of beak to the tip of tail, the glossy sleek plumage, the economy of movement. He would find nothing like it in peacocks, ducks, sparrows or magpies. Crows were perfect.

When his thoughts returned to Pjotr, he realized how much he knew about this man's criminal business and violent character; That he would not hesitate to take the needed talent by force. He felt it better to leave town. Musing, he turned the golden ring on his finger, then rose and walked away.

1

Pjotr cursed Eugen all the way to his limousine and dropped into the rear. His heart was hammering, his mind ranting: *Rotten bastard. Ditched me like dirt. I'll wring your neck. Touted a theory. Ha. Maundered of millions. Cranky nut. Didn't even look at my diamonds.*

"Katworski!"

The chauffeur headed to the cocktail bar, where Pjotr would get tanked. The bar man wondered about his regular at this early hour, who obviously was not in the mood for a soft starter. No Singapore Sling as usual. He poured him a glass of Swiss Highland Single Malt Whiskey, put it before him with a *cheers Pjotr* and placed the bottle next to it.

Slowly, Pjotr calmed down trying to make sense of Eugen's behavior. *What makes him tick these days,* he thought, *anything I have missed of late?*

Pjotr remembered Eugen's ring which he had seen again today – this chunky ring of the heroes of the Soviet Union – hammer and sickle in gold on red.

Memories now overwhelmed him. There was a scene – burned into his memory, which had haunted his dreams for years – an image he could not push aside. He saw himself among the large audience at the Kremlin's Palace of Congress, when Eugen, decorated with the ring and a medal and hailed by the crowd, had stepped down from the stage and the spotlights. An orchestra in a sea of flowers had played for him and an admiral of the Arctic Fleet had praised him, the comrade superstar of robotics.

Until then, robotics had received little attention. The USSR favored more spectacular technology like satellites, submarines or rockets – symbols of greatness, strength and dominance. So robots, a new class of systems lay aside – a class of inconspicuous machines which went their own way.

But Eugen's robots passed their test splendidly and kicked the country to the scientific forefront. Dispatched in the Baltic Sea, these autonomous diving vehicles explored the naval facilities of Sweden, operating entirely on their own. No one could have steered them through the cliffs of the coast, to find submarine plants and bunkers.

Despite all former reconnaissance via spies and satellites, pretty little was known about the Swedish naval forces. Thus, when Eugen's robots delivered exquisite findings, it came like a shock – unexpected and inexplicable. The Party soon learned about the first autonomous device behind the Iron Curtain – the scientific breakthrough of Eugen, the genius. And Eugen joined the heroes of the Soviet Union.

Pjotr groaned, bearing the brunt of memories. He had been proud of his friend at the lyceum. He had come all the way from Siberia to congratulate him and celebrate him, had brought a rare bottle of Grusinian Kognak, once Stalin's favorite drink.

Pjotr savored the lavish celebrations at the institute. He experienced how passionately the team adored Eugen and admired the ingenious functional design, which implemented the robot's intelligence.

These memories hurt. Pjotr bit his lip, spit blood. What Eugen had brought to life many years ago, was priceless now.

Yet an hour ago, Eugen had scorned his generous offer. Why on earth hadn't he accepted? Pjotr was at a loss and drank. Later, he began to think about his options: *Money? Money was out. Eugen didn't care. Sex? No, he would not fall for that either. But Eugen would cooperate if he learned about the threats – the methods of the mafia. They worked miracles. Always.* Pjotr emptied the bottle with a smirk.

2

Chuck read a message on his cell phone, slammed the door shut and went down to the lobby to meet Bill, his guest. Relieved, he faced the great old man.

„You have come. So, you trusted me. I am glad indeed to see you after all these years."

„To tell the truth, I could not remember you, just had the feeling *this guy is ok*. You could have given me a hint. What's up?"

„I'll tell you the whole story – on a little excursion, if you agree."

„Which way?"

„Down the Potomac, then we'll have lunch and talk in peace and quiet."

When Bill nodded, Chuck signaled the receptionist to have the car brought around. Soon they were off, recalling old times, 25 years past, when Chuck had joined Bill's team.

Bill had managed a CIA-project which had failed before: espionage via satellite, the first super telescope in orbit, films of unimagined high resolution and a novel transfer of information between a satellite and CIA headquarters. The technology fascinated Chuck, then at the beginning of his career. A roll of film was catapulted from the satellite, descended on parachute, was intercepted in mid-air over the Pacific Ocean by a special jet plane and immediately transferred to Washington DC.

Likewise fascinated, Chuck observed Bill's management: how he formed and led a superior team. He calmly handled the most critical situations. Nobody could trick him with sugar coated numbers. He knew the details of the project – studied them in eary mornings. He sensed the team's mood and – this was a rare gift – he recognized and acknowledged good work.

Soon after his project was done, Bill had retired to lead a private life, caring for his sick wife. Chuck had lost track but remembered him as one of the few great and noble men he had ever known.

At the marina, they stepped into Chuck's boat, drove down the river, disembarked at *Granny's Crabcakes,* a little restaurant on the eastern bank, sat down at a table under mighty sycamore trees and looked over the wide waters. At this beautiful spot, Bill enjoyed the outing.

„Now,enough suspense. What's on your mind?"

„I am on a mission from Terry Hancock, Security Adviser to the President."

Terry had seen the dangers of terror. But he distrusted national agencies entirely; the three secret services above all. He was concerned:

„They are stuck, blindly crunching masses of data. *Echelon* started the Cold War misery in Bavaria and England by tapping radio transmissions large scale. Every year I hear the same hackneyed patter: the volume of data doubles, thus the budget must triple.

It had been just like that during the Cold War. When the Communists had had 6000 nuclear war heads, they said we need twice as many. Today they want server farms and supercomputers.
But sightless, mindless nuts they are: always on the same old track and speeding in the wrong direction. They never notice."
Terry invited Chuck and his team and stated the task:

„Our security machinery constitutes an enormous risk. In six years it will hit the wall. The Israelis take a different approach – probably smarter – and the Chinese as well.

If we ignore the smart solution, then help us God. Now get to work. Grind out ideas. I want new options."

In the meantime, Bill had finished his dessert.

„Now tell me, finally, what are you going to do?"

„I want you on board. Please put a team together."

Bill was not amused.

„Nonsense. I am an old man who enjoys Granny's chocolate fudge sheba in the shade."

„You are the right one."

„I know nothing about terror."

„Back then you knew nothing about satellites except that rockets launch them. And yet it was you who put things on track again.

„I don't know anyone any more, my contacts have rusted."

„We'll oil them. We got money."

„Have you also got an idea?"

„Not really. Just, the other day I ran across a book I devoured as a boy: *The Hound of the Baskervilles*. I read it again and marveled at Sherlock Holmes once more. He made me think."

„Ah, you want to create a detective like him?"

„One? Hundreds perhaps. Some intelligent counterpoint to the foolish things done by the agencies. But for now, it is nothing but a fancy idea."

Bill rose.

„Hm. A fancy idea? I listened to you. Now I am tired. Let's go back."

Back at the marina, Bill shook hands with a faint smile:

„Come and see me in my Virginia home sometime soon."

3

Chuck drove down to the Shenandoah Valley, up the hill to Bill's home and parked next to the stables, which had once housed Susan's horses.

Bill put an arm around Chuck's shoulders and pushed him into the simple kitchen of the country-style house. They sat down at the table in front of the large window and looked to the Appalachian Mountains in the mist as they had pizza and coffee. Then, before the sun began to sink behind the hills, Bill led his guest past the white fence of an empty paddock, upward to a point where they could see the river and park in the valley. Bill came often to this peaceful scenic place he had named *Susan's Vista*.

On the way back, Bill talked about himself. After Susan's death, he had sold the horses. He did it with a heavy heart, since horses had been part of his life when he rode to school as a boy, but their sale made time to do things he loved.

With pleasure he continued Susan's honorary office in the National Park nearby. History, too – the American evolution induced by the Civil War – attracted and absorbed him. He and his friends founded the Association for the Research on General Robert E. Lee.

Obviously, Bill didn't need another job. Chuck's wish to build and manage a team would strain the old man, steal his leisure time and rob him of his strength. Chuck asked him just the same.

Bill didn't answer but led him to a huge smooth boulder in front of the house. Susan had loved it and had used to dance on it in the morning sun.

„I'll do it for her. Susan would have wanted it. More than anything she cared for freedom."

Slowly Bill stepped onto the rock.

„I stood right here on this spot when I scattered her ashes in a storm. Then I smashed the urn. She wanted it this way, wanted to be free even in death. One of these days, Chuck, the wind will take my ashes, too, and take them to her."

Now, they turned to the house. Bill had spoken about his wife, his hobbies and his motivation, had spoken about things he wanted Chuck to know. Chuck wasn't surprised – Bill was exactly how he figured him: an old-fashioned patriot who lived for his convictions and ideals. *He serves America with pleasure*, he thought in relief.

„Come inside, let's have dinner – steak and beans is today's menu. I cooked that when I was a boy on our farm in Texas."

During dinner, they discussed the hurdle they had to overcome, else the project wouldn't get off the ground.

They could not travel the country heralding their vague vision to universities, research labs and industries, scouting for ideas on what to do. Just as well, they could trust a fox to keep the geese. The project was dead if they lifted the cloak of secrecy but a little.

Years ago, Bill had had it easier despite his top-secret job. Back then the CIA had spoiled him, now it would crush him would it find out about his plans. Times had changed in many ways. Then, he was not permitted to travel abroad, not even to visit his sister in Munich which lay much too close to the Iron Curtain.

Tomorrow he would have to travel the world, visit places not yet infested by the NSA. Chuck warned him of the Israelis and the English, the old guard – he wouldn't be safe there. India, on the other hand, seemed to be OK and technically fit since many Indians had relocated after a career in the US.

And there was also France, where he would find top scientists and friendship. The French – not the government but the ordinary people – had presented the American people with the Statue of Liberty, a grandiose gift. And the heroic US-boys who kicked the Nazis out of the country remained unforgotten in France. The French were friends minding their own thing, which is to say: the Grande Nation kept the NSA at bay and off its territory.

"Chuck, let's savor a bottle in honor of the French. I hope you will like this *Entre Deux Mers*, a fine Merlot. It comes, by the way, with a story. Susan and I once toured the Bordeaux region on bicycle and got lost for good. At night and utterly exhausted we found a solitary chateau, which cultivates this wine. Seeing Susan almost in tears, the vintner welcomed us, prepared a bed, gave us his ham and bread and a bottle of wine. We were in paradise. Never tasted wine so good and ever since we have served this wine on special occasions.

They tasted the wine and went on to dicuss another crux of the matter. They guessed they would need cutting edge technology they knew little about: computers, networks and software. But unless they had a more precise goal and an idea of a technical solution, they could not begin to recruit experts. Expertise, however, was already needed to devise anything of value. Bill worried:

„The dog seems to chase its tail. I hope the wine doesn't forebode evil. Are we caught *entre deux mers* which means *between two seas*?

Talking, they emptied another bottle. Both of them knew people well-versed with computers and the Internet, but could not sound them out. They had to disguise their objectives and invent a cover. Bill, for instance, could act incognito, equipped with a new identity.

Finally they decided on a way out of the problem. Chuck would set up a foundation for social research bestowed with the best of references. As the foundation's president, Bill would mimic a wealthy philanthropist, feign interest, and discuss exotic projects. Everyone would trust this great old man and many would adore him.

Chuck's calculations reached only this far. Bill was the only one who could play this role, and he would play along. Yet, it was a risky game, Russian roulette if Chuck ditched Terry Hancock.

Chuck and Bill, the old hands, were quite aware of their situation, but went to bed upbeat. The *Chateau de Soussac* had taken effect.

4

Eugen, hero of bygone days, lived a retired life in a changing world. Leningrad had re-gained its old name *St. Petersburg* and the shops were brimming with western goods he could not afford. He watched luxury cars while waiting for busses which did not arrive, and occasionally the heating of his flat failed. From his point of view, Russia was ailing and not even former heroes could trust its care.

His award had brought him fame, contacts and even modest funds, which is why he didn't have to rough it. He enjoyed an independent life, possessing what he needed most: a piano and computers. Most of his neighbors enjoyed his wit and liked him. A few considered him a Bohemian, though no one ever found him drunk, but rumor had it he dealt with strange things – robots.

Robots made him a longtime client of the black market where he hunted for rare spare parts as well as for microchips from Japan and the US. He rarely paid for them, because the black market merchants valued his expert tips more than money.

Eugen relied on Feiwel, once this market's best organizer, because robots demanded the latest in technology. Components made in the USSR were too big, too heavy and slow and their power consumption a nightmare. Even products of Robotron, the GDR champion, didn't serve him. He owed his success to US companies as well as to Feiwel who always found a way to trick the communist system and supply the desired products of Digital Equipment Corporation und Texas

Instruments. With time, Feiwel became one of Eugen's few friends – one who had risked jail and the Gulag for the robots.

Today, nobody gave a damn anymore for the Swedish navy and the robots were outmoded. This chapter closed, Eugen savored being his own master, playing the music he loved on the piano and Feiwel's hacking game on the computer. The rules of Feiwel's game were simple. Each week they lunched together and – over dessert – Feiwel chose a target computer. Then the race was on: whoever managed to break into it first won and didn't have to pay for next week's lunch.

Hacking was fun, but merely an excercise. Eugen's true passion lay elsewhere: he devoted his time and energy to advance his theory of machine intelligence. This theory had reached the stage of development comparable to the state of aviation in 1930: already functioning and moving on an undreamed-of future when people would fly at any time to any place.

Eugen knew that through his work on marine robots he had found golden nuggets, essential parts of his theory, but not yet the grand prize, if there was one. He was experienced enough to realize that his theory still had a long way to go. Indeed, the challenge was frightening and he was struggling badly, being all by himself.

Then Pjotr called him out of the blue, trying to establish contact after many years of silence, talking about the times they spent at the lyceum, asking how he was.

This call caused a turn-about: it made Eugen's thoughts wander back in time and remember his class at the lyceum located at the fringe of the Ural, decades ago. He remembered Pjotr, the strange kids, Svetlana, his first love and comrade Siebenlist, the only teacher he adored. They found out the German name *Siebenlist* meant *seven ploys* but called him *Sevenchicks*, because he had seven daughters. He seemed to loathe the Communist dogma worshipped by all other teachers, and to love ideas which were not in the textbooks.

Suddenly many things came to mind about Siebenlist: he had to have *torte* every day, and sometimes referred to strange people like Albert Camus and Aristotle which caused a stir at the school. *This man*, Eugen thought, *tried to introduce me to ancient thinking to lay the foundation for modern thought. And I did not grasp it then.* Then, Eugen remembered that Siebenlist had told him about Aristotle's ancient categories. *This is important* he said, looking me in the eyes, *You hear me? Important! I don't care for the other buggers in class, but you, Eugen, must study that.*

Eugen swore he would honor his liquidated mentor and catch up on those unknown categories after all. When this happened he felt he struck gold.

He saw at once that categories were a powerful means to organize knowledge. His robots had to know a lot about the Baltic Sea, about their own capabilities, about Sweden's submarines, mine-sweepers, speedboats and frigates. They also had to know their mission and goals and how to deliver the findings. This knowledge base was enormous and growing day by day. It was also complex and tended to become convoluted and, thus, un-reliable. Knowledge, Eugen learned, was a very special thing and by no means a mere accumulation of facts. It had to be structured and ordered, but how? Categories looked promising.

The three categories *Thing*, *Qualitiy* and *Quantity* appealed to Eugen right away, because they named and distinguished fundamental aspects. They demanded that Things like Eugen himself be kept apart from Qualities like being Russian or Quantities like weighing 80 kg.

Things, qualities and quantities had nothing in common. A thing may have a quality but could never be a quality. Knowledge about things, qualities and quantities, therefore, had better be kept apart. Eugen loved the fact that when searchning a knowledge base for a person he had to look for a thing only, not for a quantity or location or action or else. *Wow, how handy this is*, Eugen thought, *categories order knowledge*.

Then Eugen took a break and flew south to hike on the soft slopes of mount Ararat. He had to be alone, clear his mind and think about categories. He did not know how to find the many categories he would need nor how to use them to their full potential.

He was on his own. Western scientists had never dealt with this topic. And here at the foot of the mountain, he was alone with shepherds and sheep.

Finally a vision formed which intrigued him and pushed him on. Wistfully he thought of his handpicked team at the institute. It could have worked for years implementing his new theory, a matchless task promising fame and glory and the noblest prizes.

Eugen believed in his theory. But how to implement it, test it and prove it worked? Building systems for universal learning and universal problem-solving was a Herculean task. Too much for him to accomplish alone.

He needed help, but doubted he would find it in the remainder of the USSR, and not even in the west.

Two decades ago, the challenge to build machines of super-human intelligence lured the best brains in the west and let them fail. When finally the man who argued that such machines could never exist won an award, a once-booming scientific discipline came to an end. Funding stopped and the teams dissolved.

Eugen knew about this western crisis of Artificial Intelligence. He had closely followed the American research thanks to the Ministry of Foreign Trade that provided him with western books and journals. Then, he learned the English language with pleasure, even loved its free and optimistic spirit. More, still, he loved the spirit of western music. Charlie Parker's Jazz opened to him a world beyond imagination.

5

Eugen was under way to get rid of his computers. *Feiwel's ICT – Components Devices Tools* was engraved on the metal plate at the door of a shop which had been a meeting place of insiders and a forum for rumors, hints and ideas. Now, the shop looked like as a museum and an oriental bazaar, offering yesterday's Soviet technology as well as tinker-ware of many sorts. Feiwel was doing badly since the fans of old technology were dying off, but it had not always been like this. Feiwel belonged to a large family, a brother who worked with the Telecom of Cyprus and an uncle who helped develop the Arpanet in the US.

Feiwel once benefitted from a very particular circumstance because the German government and industry pushed business in the east. Siemens, for instance, supplied the Soviets with a Center for Production and Automation in the Ural Mountains. It therefore complied with the wishes of the Ministry of Foreign Trade by installing a communication link between Moscow and Cyprus. The ministry chose Siemens because it had been active in the Middle East for generations, connecting countries via telegraph, telex and telephone networks. Now it was replacing analog telephony with digital technology.

Eugen noticed with interest that a modern digital telephone switch was set up in Moscow and linked to Bulgaria and further on via radio to Cyprus. Some Soviet courier service was using this link into the west.

He had tipped Feiwel off: modern communication networks were remotely controlled – a handy feature. If Feiwel managed to enter the Cyprus switch, he would be able to configure the Moscow switch. Then a way to the west would open and treasures come within reach: technical specifications, processors, sensors, actors and more. Couriers could be bribed and Feiwel and his brother would profit.

Soon after, Eugen and Feiwel established their private connection into the west using a device which appears prehistoric today: a portable terminal made by TI. It was able to connect to computers – if only slowly – simply by placing a telephone handset onto it and let it dial into a certain network – thus connecting St. Petersburg to Silicon Valley. From this day on, Feiwel struck gold and Eugen was served.

The Taxi stopped in front of Feiwel's ICT and Eugen unloaded workstations to deposit them at his friend's. Feiwel welcomed him:

„Wow. Moving?"

„Just traveling, my friend. But this time I must take care. They will break into my flat, hunting for these machines. But they shall find nothing. See these sticks and CDs here. They are for your strongbox. Keep my softare jewels well."

„Who would want your boxes? Pretty exotic stuff, all home-made, I figure. Nobody else buys what you are buying from me."

„A talented guy could read my technical design and get ideas which I prefer to keep to myself. Feiwel, if you want to cannibalize my boxes, please do so. They are yours now. When I return, I'll build new ones."

While Feiwel put the computers away, Eugen rummaged in drawers and boxes. He knew the place. But Feiwel objected.

„Not here – that's the old stuff."

„But it's what I am looking for. I want presents."

"Video processors?"

"And sensors for pressure, temperature, inclination, acceleration. They must have a slow interface to fit a weak processor."

„Hey, look at that, a vintage signal processor. You used one like it for your crows."

„What's the serial number? Ah, the wrong charge, not for the military. But ok, I'll take it anyway."

Feiwel looked at Eugen's rum collection of components and shook his head. Eugen had always been good for a surprise, but these antiques? Crazy. Then Eugen paid and slapped Feiwel on the back.

„So long, my friend."

Feiwel hugged him:

„If you are not back soon, I'll check youre flat, I still got the keys. Take care now. And drop me a line."

6

The Chaos Communication Camp is an international, four-day open-air event for hackers and associated life-forms. The Camp features lectures, workshops and experiments.

You can participate! Bring your tent and join our village. The Camp takes place 7/8/9/10th July near Berlin, Germany (Old Europe).

Hordes of hackers followed this invitation as they had in the years before. The camp lay amidst Brandenburg's pretty countryside, bordered by fields, paddocks and a lake.

A transmission mast towered over tents and stalls, trucks and generators, servers and the tangle of cables. This was no place unlike any other. It was home to a tight-knit group of people. English, Dutch, Polish and German voices were in the air. Many enjoyed the camp's peaceful morning after a busy night at the computer. Others like Jean and Wacko kept the organization going, knitting the electric network. Kids met at the chippy and in the seminar tent and were turned on by the hundreds of new ideas that went around the camp. But only at night by the glow of small lamps and by the sound of saxophone and bongo, the magic of the camp unfolded.

7

People rushed and pushed and sounds filled the air: *Eugen, Eugen, hello professor, hi buddy...* Campers surrounded Eugen who had arrived, tired, smiling, and welcome at a familiar site.

The newbies quickly learned about the commotion: *the Russian Guru ... a true genius ... from St. Petersburg ... analyzed the RPS Codes ... is the best.* Jean and Wacko dropped the cables to embrace Eugen, but someone had already dragged him into a tent. Moments later Eugen sat in front of a screen, absorbed in a problem.

It was Eugen's destiny to be dragged from tent to tent, confronted with computers day and night. That's why he was here – to absorb the ideas of the kids, the professionals and the freaks, and to share his wisdom with everyone. Spellbound fans crowded around him talking a strangely cryptic idiom: *why skip single sign on? ... ran into authentication failure ...can't generate random challenge ...crypto calc now ...no, new SRV type ...sniffer like Carnivore.*

They had fun joking about all that went wrong – hacks that failed and robots that misbehaved. Özi, still only a boy, let his little robot roll, a weird contraption of wheels, wires and electronic components. Slowly it moved along the edge of the table when one of the onlookers shook a bunch of keys in front of its sensors. Like being scared, the vehicle reversed, went over the edge and dropped into Özi's lap. It raised laughter and jeer: *Can't teach him table manners? Off to mom's lap. Beddy-by, beauty.* The camp was a jolly place.

8

Strolling thru the camp, Eugen found Özi deep in thought in front of his old PC.

„Hi, my friend. Doing well?“

Proudly, Özi presented his work. His robot rolled through the gap between two bottles barely wide enough. Eugen observed the precise maneuver with interest then slapped the boy on the back.

"Wow, sensor coupling is great."

As Özi beamed with joy, Eugen sat down next to him. They talked about interfaces of sensors and the narrow-chested processor in the robot. Then questions of architecture came up: how to optimize costs, energy consumption, computing power and function surveillance. At last, Eugen checked the hardware:

„I guess, your processor is too weak for modern sensors. Old ones are better. Try these!"

Eugen pulled two sensors and a CD from his backpack, slipped them to Özi with a nobody-needs-to-know-squint. Then he continued to Wacko's tent.

Wacko, an old school hacker looked like a left-over hippie with long hair and beard, adorned with chains, tattoos and piercings. He and Jean brooded over the outcome of their experiment. They tried – like most others in the camp – to win CSC, the Chemical Systems Contest: 20,000 dollars for the computer wizard who broke into a tamper-proof phenol synthesis plant.

They had reached a dead end and knew why. Being at their wit's end they cursed the system, ready to give up. When Eugen mentioned the premise for a solution, Wacko snubbed him:

„Oh indeed? But you can't trick this trusted server. A guy like you should know that."

After a pause, Eugen broke the silence of the stumped round.

„I'll try."

Wacko turned to him, miffed.

„Bullshit … don't bullshit me … damn."

„Want to bet?"

Wacko paused in disbelief. Would Eugen try the impossible? Then he checked the odds: no-one in the camp would even bother to think about this job, the entire hackerscene had given up. He smirked and agreed.

„Ok. How much?"

Eugen turned the ring around the finger and bet for much more money than he had with him. He produced a CD and started a program, letting thousands of lines scroll down the screen. When the program finally stopped, it showed a single line. Wacko and Jean realized with a glance that the server had reacted the way Eugen wanted. He had won.

They fell silent for a while – overwhelmed and perplexed. At last, Jean found his speech again.

„All locks broken, all doors forced open. Oh my god. It's the dawn of a new age."

Wacko and Jean felt paralyzed, didn't talk. Finally, Wacko reached up to the bizarre collection of plush toys hanging from the top of the tent, reached into the back of a giant teddy bear, pulled out a wad of money and put it into Eugen's hand. Uncounted, Eugen pocketed his winnings, signaled them to keep things secret and left.

Up to now, Eugen had never allowed anyone to take such a close look at his bag of tricks. But he was pinched for money and loved to see the pundits gape in amazement. This time his illegal trick had gone too far but he feared no repercussion, although the news would spread like wildfire though the camp. He had left no trace. But he had made Jean think.

An American had visited Jean the other day; a strange fellow and an impressive globetrotter who told the most amusing tales of bygone times. He even made Jean philosophize about the power and the menace of the Internet. Jean couldn't make sense of the America's intentions, a man who looked around the institute, talked about cooperation and seemed to favor strange types and tasks. In any case, he had money.

9

Jean led Eugen across the meadows along the paddocks, heading for the lake. He patted horses while talking about the farm where he grew up.

„When the harvest was done, we butchered a pig. Nothing else is burned more into my memory. The butcher, family and friends were busy from dawn on and at noon we sat together feasting on pork boiled in the large kettle. By evening the sausages were in the smoke and the ham in the salt.

You see, I grew up in the sticks. I love the place and would have stayed if we had had a bigger farm.

Come along with me down to the Drôme and see the farm for yourself. You'll love the place too."

Eugen had no need to hurry home and agreed right away, though he had never heard of the Drôme. While they were approaching the lake, he thought of the flat Russian province where he once had volunteered in a harvesting brigade. He remembered the fleet of tractors on endless fields and the odd charm of the kolkhoz. It didn't lure anybody, but France lured him. Friends used to rave about its virtues: cuisine, culture, and climate.

After a while Jean got down to business. He wanted to win Eugen over to work for the renowned *French Institute for the Security of Computer Networks*, where he led a department. They discussed the mammoth and all-too-obvious challenges of network protection. The aggressors seemed to always be a step ahead and would always stay ahead. Eugen's spectacular trick in the camp had proven this fact once more.

Internet hardware and software as they were today could never guarantee security. Jean, envisioned a radically new network architecture which required new networks built from scratch.

He knew very well this vision would remain a daydream only. *New networks,* Eugen thought, *what an insane idea.* He looked at Jean and saw he had given up hope.

„Eugen, I want to be candid – I am scared of the future. You and I have witnessed paradise: the Internet of old. It was boundless and free, democratic and promising – the symbol of a brave new era. But now it's down and out, it's an ugly instrument for sex and crime."

At the lake Eugen sat down on a bench, looking around for a while, taking in the soft atmosphere of the countryside, feeling its peace and quiet. St. Petersburg seemed endlessly removed. Then Jean came up to him again:

„Eugen, our institute attracts hackers like flies. We try hard to protect our stronghold, but it will fall. It's only a matter of time.

Did you know that 5 million people live in France whose roots are in Algeria, Morocco and the Sahel? They are honorable people, but there are also extremists. Eugen, they threatened me."

„Don't worry, my friend. The extremists will win a battle or two, but they will not win the arms race. Remember, first there were clubs, then bows and arrows, next guns and cannons, tanks and bombers. Man devised an antidote for each of them."

„But we have no antidote. We are desperate. Eugen, will you help us?"

10

Soon after, they were under way. Jean took a scenic route through Bavaria and Switzerland, past Lake Geneva into the Savoy. Here he left the highway to drive on little roads south to the Maurienne, an El Dorado of cyclists. He wanted to show Eugen three legendary mountain passes and his heart beat faster. Eugen watched in silence.

On the Col de la Madeleine the view extended north to the giant glaciers of the Mont Blanc and south to a sea of Alpine peaks. Eugen had imagined France a small, soft country, studded with castles where gentle people cultivate the best wine in the world. Long ago, he had read this in a book about Napoleon's wars.

They continued – up the Col de la Croix de Fer and on through scraggy, lofty mountains – up to the Col du Galibier, king of mountain passes of the Tour de France. Racing bikes glittered in the sun and resting bikers looked at the glacial scarps of Les Ecrins, just a mile away. Jean pointed down to where the road bent.

„I used to bike up at dawn before the race. You see the bend? There I waited when the race came from the north. Before this turn the racers toil up a brutal ramp and whoever wins the ramp, wins the race. There, I screamed my head off for my heroes."

Then they rolled down the pass following the river Romanche towards the foothills of the Alps. And again Jean talked about his worries:

„Believe me, the hacker-pest will soon run riot and become pandemic. I am still shocked by your hack."

„It won't be as bad as that. The threats are monumental, to be sure. And our defense is shaky, in that you are correct as well. But it's not the end. There are new ideas, new routes to follow. And now I am going to tell you about things you may know little about."

Eugen sketched the times around 1970, when machines began to compute fast enough for something a handful of researchers had thought up and called Artificial Intelligence. They stopped to command computers to *do this, next that*. Instead they began to feed them with facts about the world and a logical calculus, to derive new facts from given ones.

Some such ideas had been dreamt of in the Middle Ages but now computers were programmed to compose music, invent stories and play chess. But most of all, machines could absorb the knowledge of experts. And indeed they learned from the best physicians – how to treat a patient's stumbling heart by applying Digitalis, a toxic drug.

Computers should learn day and night, absorb all the facts of an encyclopedia, and much more.

It was a time of pioneers, researchers of the mind. And it was the time of big money and Cold War strategies. Hundreds of millions of dollars flowed into the temples of science and research. Defense strategists envisioned quantum leaps of technology, yielding smart robots for instance, smart missiles and more.

Back then, machines rarely had sufficient knowledge to perform their tasks well. That is why a program invented a children's story in which gravity died. Gravity's death was a logical consequence of a jumping dog. As the dog jumped, gravity pulled him down. So both, the dog and gravity, happened to land in water. The program knew that animals, therefore dogs, could swim, but not gravity. Bad luck, thus, for gravity. It had to drown – according to the simple rule: all objects which cannot swim in water must sink, thus drown. The program knew very little about gravity: was it an object like a dog or else?

Eugen: „You see, the deficits of Artificial Intelligence were enormous, surpassed only by the hype about some early achievements.

Back then I built a robot which scouted the Swedish coast all by itself. It spotted chances to act, watched for risks, set goals, made plans, performed tasks, and so on. It even checked itself: *How did I do my job?* Thanks to this feature, called introspection, it became a clever beast.

Jean, I am telling you this old lore because we must be clever as well, must build a smart defense. Of course, the Internet has no need for diving robots. But think of truly smart Internet-watchers, intelligent rangers protecting your institute. They will be made of software of a very different kind."

They left the Alps at last. Jean halted the car on top of a hill where he unpacked wine, bread and cheese on a blanket.

„Look around. You are *en Drôme*, almost at home. Let's picnic."

Soft green hills, *Les Collines*, lay around them. To the east they saw the great white peaks of the High Alps, where they had come from. In the West, vineyards stretched to the valley of the Rhône and to the hills beyond the mighty river. Down in the valley rested the old Abbey Saint Antoine – what a sight. Jean pointed south.

„That's where we'll go. We are close now."

Jean drove along a wall of artfully stacked boulders covered by blooming smartweed, then turned through an open gate and stopped in front of an old farmhouse.

„Voilà Eugen, you are home."

The door opened and Anna stepped down the stairs, her hair carefully done, wearing no makeup, a plain dress and delicate shoes. Jean ran up to his mother and kissed her cheeks. Eugen, feeling crinkled after the days in camp, remained shy as Anna turned to him.

„You must be Eugen – Jean called ahead. Bienvenue, feel welcome."

An old tractor drove by clamorously and Jean waved to the driver.

„It's Henri, our neighbor, who does the farming. You will meet him.

I'll be off to my family now, but will come and see you in a few days. Until then, have fun my friend. Salut."

Anna led Eugen into the farm's long hallway, decorated only by the head of a wild boar and the portrait of a hunter next to it, and explained:

„This fancy decoration reminds us of the blessed animal which kept my father from starvation in hard times."

She gently pushed him with an *enter my realm* into her kitchen.

„You must be hungry and I have a snack for you."

Eugen took a deep breath and Anna smiled.

„Old kitchens smell, mine does too."

„And what a pleasant smell it is," Eugen said, looking around, taken in by a homey sight – the auburn tiles on the floor, the dark joists on the ceiling and the bunches of herbs on the wall. He liked it and he showed it.

Anna pointed to bottles stacked in an alcove.

„It's our wine. You'll like it. You are lucky, the cherries are ripe and the first tomatoes. Take a seat now and taste them."

On the way to his room, Eugen walked by Anna's parlor. As he spotted a piano his heart jumped.

He passed his days playing the piano and exploring a new world – French composers, Henri's old tractor, Anna's garden and her library. Anna watched amused, while he studied her exotic books.

„You read Aristotle? In Greek?"

„I teach his philosophy and I love it. It's my privilege."

„Marxism is the only philosophy I know. If you'd call Marx a philosopher."

„In any case, Marx learned from the famous philosopher Georg Wilhelm Friedrich Hegel. So don't be afraid of philosophy."

12

A few days later, Jean and his mother were sitting on the bench in the garden behind the house. Jean was fond of this place among the berries and apricots he had loved to pick as a boy.

„Now, what do you think of Eugen, maman? I am curious."

„He responds to the charm of the Drôme. I can feel it. He likes our wine and the cherries a lot. He already met Henri and came back with dirty hands."

„Henri told me that Eugen came to see him. They could not converse, so they tinkered with the tractor. Eugen should come again, he said."

„There you go. The other day Eugen walked all the way to St. Antoine. When he came back, he could not hear enough about the abbey. So, I told him about St. Antoine, the hermit. We were sitting here, on this bench. He had no idea what a relic was. Ha. He could not believe that people revered a splinter of a hermit's bone. And he wondered about its odyssey: that first the Egyptians had it, then the Arabs, then the Byzantines robbed it and a French knight brought it home, where the church finally got it. He thought I was telling him a kind of fairy tale."

„Was he interested in history?"

41

„Not really. What really interested him were the monks. How could it be that a small bunch of people built a monastery, a church and even a hospital? *What made these guys so strong*, he asked, but I didn't know."

„When we talked on the phone, he mentioned a scary experience."

„True. I took him on a scenic trip up to the Grands Goulets. We parked in front of the giant crack in the mountain where the water is rushing through and tumbling down.

But then and there, a thunderstorm came down on us. We were so scared we fled into the little dark tunnel. The lightning was blinding and the thunder deafening. My god, we seemed to be in the middle of it and my hair was standing on end. Eugen spoke of a primordial eerie beauty as the sun shone again and mist welled up the chasm."

Jean kissed his mother.

„Thanks maman, you couldn't have done better. It means so much to me. We have not yet decided on his employment."

„What's the problem?"

„We are waiting for his papers to arrive from St. Petersburg. They must be approved by the administration and the President of the Institute and, finally, the Ministry of Foreign Affairs has to agree. It will take weeks before I can make him an offer."

Anna laughed.

„Oh, I understand: safety rules the game."

„I do hope the American acts faster. He will arrive next week."

„O.k. then. I will take care of Eugen in the meantime."

„Please keep him on board. Only you can do it.“

13

Eugen stepped through the portal into the abbey's court. Today, he would meet the announced visitor, Jean's partner. A wiry, casually clad man in his late seventies walked up to him and grabbed his hand.

„Hello, you must be Eugen. I am Bill, an American. I have heard a bit about you. Great to meet you at last in this wonderful spot. Why don't we take a little walk and look around.“

They circled the abbey and took a break on a hill – the monastery spreading below them.

„Jean talked to you about his problems and you sketched a solution, which he thinks is hot. Now, let me hear it.”

„Well, it is somewhat out of the ordinary.“

„And how is this?“

While Eugen explained his approach, Bill tried to fathom Eugen's personality. He did it by playing the *I-am-you-game*. Bill had invented this game as a boy and still played it.

He imitated the other person in his mind, silently mimicking his or her conversation and movements – voicing the same words with the same emphasis and rhythm. In his mind now he raised the hands, turned the head, paused and breathed exactly like Eugen did – trying to feel him and sense his peculiarities. Bill relied on this very personal experience. As for Eugen, he had a good feelingabout him. At least this guy seemed competent.

Bill: „If we choose your solution, we choose an enormous task. We will toil and struggle."

Eugen nodded:

„Like the St. Antoine monks of old."

„I heard they were fighting a disease, a deadly inflammation, which was the terror of their times. Eugen, I feel like one of them."

They hiked back, walked through the church, looked up to the arches of the nave needing repair, climbed down to the small and somber crypt and were alone. Eugen examined the archaic place of roughly hewn rock, his hand touching the cool, strong stone.

Eugen: „Built by monks – what a team.

They were devoted to a powerful idea. Bill, only a grand idea can form a grand team. You, too, will need a grand idea."

Grand idea – the words echoed and resounded in the rocky crypt like Eugen's credo.

Days later, Bill and Eugen went for a walk to get to know each other. They hiked up to a scenic view above the *Col de la Battaille*, then down to a little lake.

Eugen learned that Bill had left behind a career as a research manager and lately committed to create a special team for a special task.

Bill learned that as a boy, Eugen had won a chess championship and suffered from it. The Communist Party made him attend a school for the gifted, far away from his mother and the music they had loved and played together. Eugen:

„They interned me in a penitentiary for kids and told me I was privileged."

„Awful, isn't it?"

„Fortunately, I had friends and my music: Tchaikovsky and Bach – enough to survive.

Once I got a recording of Charlie Parker. His Jazz was out of this world – I can still hear his music and get goose bumps. It made me feel free and feel the west. It may be the reason I am here today."

They were swimming in the lake when Bill asked the final question:

„Will you join my team?"

Eugen remembered the chances implied in Pjotr's offer. Pjotr's goals didn't intrigue him but his top team did. If he joined Pjotr, he could theorize and experiment the way he wished, and Pjotr would even push him on, since he had well understood his new tools had to be highly intelligent.

Could Bill trump this offer? Obviously, he had money and thought big. And he seemed blessed with a golden feeling for top talent. *He understands my ideas*, Eugen thought, *so I can go far*. But there was one question left: would his new colleagues understand him and go along? Finally, he responded:

„Whether I am in or not depends on our idea, the way we tackle the problem. I guess we have a chance to do an outstanding job. But we must have a team which believes in our approach."

They concluded the day in a little restaurant at the lake shore and agreed.

„Bill, I'll fly to the States and meet my colleagues. We will work out our approach and then I'll decide whether I am in or not. O.k.?"

14

A stylish jostling crowd feasted on champagne and caviar at the reception of the Russian Chamber of Commerce, a relic of the Soviet Ministry of Tourism and Foreign Trade. The Perestroika had rendered this powerful ministry obsolete, but to cultivate old contacts remained as vital for the Russian economy as the salt of the earth.

This task rested in in Aleksander's hands. Many had followed his calling to the Green Hall, a jewel of tsarist times, also called *Hall of Mercury* thanks to a ceiling fresco depicting Mercury, the god of dealers and thieves.

Ladies clad in grand robes, some in breathtaking African garb, offered a splendid sight. Pjotr amused himself all the more since the dignitaries preferred young company. Illusion meant everything at this giant rendezvous. Aleksander, self-appointed First Councilor, wore a tailcoat studded with medals of Latin American and African countries. That he had the ceiling fresco illuminated led one believe he had chosen Mercury as his godfather.

Aleksander's sweeping gesture introduced Pjotr to a Lebanese man.

„Alam, I am thrilled you have come all the long way. Be welcome, my friend. Please meet Pjotr, a specialist who will spark your interest. I hope you will amuse yourself."

It was the contact Pjotr had waited for, the key to the terror scene of the Middle East. Aleksander enjoyed extraordinary relationships – not the kind of loose contacts established during trading projects or political meetings. Most contacts dated back to the Cold War when the Soviets engaged in India, Mozambique, Angola or Cuba, deploying specialists, soldiers, secret agents, technology and spending heaps of money.

Some of the illustrious guests in the Green Hall had studied at the Lomonossow University in Moscow, others in Kiev, and had stayed in touch ever since. This old-boys-network never broke up.

Aleksander possessed the same keen sense of intentions and interpersonal affinities as the great courtesans of the baroque area. Slowly and subtly he arranged the encounter of Alam and Pjotr. Now they were talking and – seemingly inspired – exchanging business cards.

Pjotr left in the early hours of dawn and went up to his loft with a bounce in his step. Alam was a man of his taste: elegant, smart, ruthless, well connected – a man of French upbringing and yet a man of the Orient.

Three women were still up when Pjotr entered his strange abode. Nothing in the room revealed that weaving looms once roared. A glass partition allowed a glimpse of the rear rooms filled with computers – the testing ground for Pjotr's tools and innovations.

The room resembled an office, a museum and an evidence vault, displaying a crass mixture of styles. Desks and work stations were lined up close to the windows. In the center of the large room a ring of heavy chairs and couches surrounded a tall Chinese porcelain vase. Precious carpets covered the floor, Rubens paintings decorated the walls. Before them, chests, dressers and sideboards neatly closed ranks, built by masters of the Renaissance, Baroque, Rococo, Neoclas-

47

sicism, Biedermeier and Art Nouveau. On these plat-
forms stood precious pieces: candleholders and vases,
sculptures and figurines, water pipes, ivory carvings,
marquetry, porcelain dishes made in Meissen, golden
dishes made in Augsburg. The room heralded: *recognize
the man who is on top of the world.* It was Pjotr's creation
and psychogram.

Pjotr turned to the ladies:

„I had a great evening in the Green Room. We will
pull out of the banking business. You were right, my
little doves. Better business lies ahead, terror business."

He took the cognac bottle and filled the glasses.
They sat around the Chinese vase, drinking, talking and
laughing. Pjotr tried to throw a cork into the vase,
missed it and it added to the trash on the floor.

15

Back from his travels, Bill met Chuck at Crackerbarrel,
a simple restaurant where guests could keep to themselves in booths. Chuck's facial expressions revealed
tension, his gestures impatience.

„Hello headhunter, is the hunting season over? I
hope you have good news. Terry Hancock wants my
report next month."

„Yes, I got the news."

Though much of the project still lay in the dark,
the outline of a technical approach had emerged, thanks
to Jean and Eugen. It built on a bundle of Internet
technologies, security technologies, artificial intelligence, intrusion and all the other techniques employed
in the hacker scene and – this was a novelty –
computational genetics.

48

What Chuck learned from Bill's report resembled a puzzle with holes, which sketched an idea nonetheless.

Step by step, Bill had felt his way ahead. Rachel had refused his offer at first but agreed when she began to understand: Bill sought a ground-breaking mechanism to control the Internet. This she could not ignore. After all she led a renowned research facility for computer networks.

Vijay, who had recently won an international prize for computational genetics, felt uneasy since Bill's intentions remained vague and did not match his interests. But Bill didn't give in, remained stubbornly charming and promised Vijay researchers' paradise on earth.

„Look here: Eugen, Rachel and Vijay – that's the gallery of stars. That's the core of the team."

Bill showed photos and Chuck studied them intensely.

„I know Rachel, she is on several security committees and advises the NSA. What do you know about the Russian and the Indian?

Bill characterized their personalities, pointing to potential incompatibilities, and named Eugen's condition for cooperation. Chuck nodded – things were as expected. And he saw the risks – it would be one of those projects which could end in chaos.

„Let's talk about what can happen. The potential technical flaws, we'll discuss another time. Now let's look into the potential political pitfalls, since Terry is going to grill me."

Chuck had burnt his fingers once too often and made his point clear:

„There was a secret rocket of the satellite program which didn't splash down in the Pacific but banged into

Nevada – our own back yard. Something leaked, the press scented blood and went after it like a pack of wolves. Who had built the unknown rocket? For what purpose? Why didn't it appear in any budget? It must have appeared on some radar, couldn't have dodged flight control. Had the crash been hushed up? Had democratic institutions been tricked? And what did the President know?"

Chuck had been at the center of this unsavory affair, charged with protecting the CIA. He covered it up using every trick in the book: casting smoke screens, throwing people off the scent, delaying, seducing, threatening and bribing.

„Shit like that happens all the time. What if Eugen doesn't give a damn anymore? Then we must deal with a Russian who knows secret stuff and behaves as he pleases. Bill, we better watch out."

„Don't worry, I studied his character for days. I did it my way and am certain I can read him. Chuck, he is the man for us. Tell Terry, Eugen is not out for fame or riches. He pursues a unique theory. That's the focus of his life. Our project merely serves as a means to an end, though a crucial one.

I don't pretend to understand what he is up to, but it seems to me a monstrous challenge. As long as he can work on it, he will stay, which means he will stay a long time."

„Will the three prima donnas harmonize?"

„I am going to form the team around Eugen, which should not be difficult. I will take them to a simple ranch in Arizona. There, they will get to know each other and get their act together. I believe in the magic of that place. Eugen will arrive two weeks from now."

„His passport and his new identity will be ready in time. Good work, Bill."

16

Eugen prepared for his departure. One last time he helped Henri with his machinery, and one last time he sat with Anna in the garden, explaining what drove him to move to the United States. Now Jean was driving him to Saint Exupéry airport in Lyon, and soon Eugen would thank him.

Eugen had spent the time in France with pleasure. Russians always had a soft spot for this country – the artists were attracted by the parlors of Paris, the nobility by the luxury hotels at the Côte d'Azure.

With a fine sense for his Russian soul, Jean had given him a home and a family. Sophie, Jean's little daughter, had liked uncle Eugen a lot. Anna had cooked for him, *oh là là*. Even the neighbors, Marie-Thérèse and Henri came over, brought their cheese and enjoyed Tchaikovsky music on the piano.

„Jean, I hacked your machine last night. That's all I could do for you.

Certainly, the news that the French fortress of security has been broken will shock the world. So, the press will torture you, and I regret that. But keep an easy mind: you will become famous. You will be the first one to discover my new method of intrusion and understand it, too. And you will be the first to publish on the new threat for networks. So, my little misdoings won't hurt your career. *Vive la France.*"

Jean listened in utter disbelief.

„Impossible … incroyable … you tricky rascal", he stammered.

But Eugen did not pay attention, he was unwrapping a wooden puppet and handed it to Jean.

„It's my matrioshka – five dolls, one inside the other. It is as old as I am. My mother painted all of them. I hope little Sophie likes them. Thanks, my friend."

Then Eugen disappeared in the crowd.

17

Many years ago, Bill had become the second manager entrusted with a difficult task that had left his predecessor stranded. He was aware he might fail as well, but he believed a satellite camera – powerful enough to identify persons on earth – was a possibility for an outstanding team.

No doubt, his predecessor recruited outstanding engineers and physicists, but no top team emerged. Nothing had kept their colossal egos in checkand let them click into a unit which pushed itself to the limit. Its members talked about this deficit openly after they had failed and were licking their wounds.

Bill thus gathered his new team on this ranch, a place where nobody felt at home, where they would do things no one had done before and where they would have to sove problems together.

They set out at night, rode up the mountain, saw the sun rise over the desert and returned exhausted by the torrid heat. All of them dithered, all of them suffered, all were equal in the saddle.

Most every day they were underway on horseback, camped up at the barrier lake and felt like settlers on the Oregon Trail – roughing it while heading for California, the Promised Land.

It happened on one of their outings: they lost their bearings. They rested in the meager shadow of a mountain and recognized the danger. Fears and doubts were voiced. Should they rest or move on, split up or stay together? They argued passionately, having no leader and no safe way. At last they calmed down to hear the voice of an intern saying:

„Slacken the reins, guys. Trust the horses, our broncos know the way home."

Bill was playing with the dog on the veranda and thinking back to this day, when his team was born.

Now a new team would form. Eugen, Rachel and Vijay would only win as a team. They had already landed on Apache Airport and were on the road to the ranch.

Nobody lived here except a Mexican couple who cared for the guests, a few horses and the dog.

Before the dam had been built, the ranch had water, cattle and ranch hands. But when the well dried up, the ranch dwindled to a resort for those who pursue the simple life, far from the masses and the hustle.

Now Bill saw dust above the dirt road – a pickup was approaching.

18

Dressed in jeans and sneakers, Bill, Eugen, Rachel und Vijay met for supper at the big table before the fireplace. Four generations of farmers had sat around this table, and taken their guns from the wall over the door before they rode into the wild countryside. Now, the little team would venture out into unknown territory, pushing the boundaries of technology. Bill clinked his glass, rose and said:

„Friends, you are my candidates of choice, the team I had hoped for. Feel welcome. Feel the spirit of this ranch. Think of the settlers on the barren land and do like the pioneers of old: Come together. Each of you must learn to trust the others. Teams don't just happen. I want you to work for our team and work hard. And don't look to me – it's you who must form the team."

Then they sat around the cold fireplace: Eugen, Rachel, the professor for computer networks at the Massachusetts Institute of Technology on the east coast of the USA, and Vijay, the young professor of computer genetics at Stanford University on the west coast – a Russian, an American and an Indian.

Bill recommended an outing on horseback though none of them had ever ridden a horse. Now they were joking about their riding abilities.

„Rachel even broke her hobby horse – Vijay learned riding on elephants – Russians, the steppe-tribes, are born in the saddle." Thus they talked till the end of the day.

Bill left the ranch before dawn, riding in the cool of night, led by the stars as he had done before. He rested on a hill, leaned back on a rock and saw the desert as the sun was rising. Again he sensed the feeling he had had as a boy – to be lonely and free on the ranch of his parents.

Nothing spectacular was in sight from his outlook, neither the contour of hills on the far horizon nor the wind-blown rocks on the the plain. The project had troubled him, but not anymore. The vast untouched land set his mind to rest. Then he murmured: *God bless America* and rode back.

When he returned, the team was busy sketching ideas and testing each other's abilities: expertise, creativity and leadership.

Would they be able to counter the dangers of terror they had witnessed a thousand fold and still could not nail down?

What if all the weirdoes of the Chaos Communication Club joined forces against those who dominated the Internet reaping fortunes? Eugen recalled the slogan at the club: *Who sets the net free? You & me!*

What if a Terror State controlled the Internet? How would it happen and how could they prevent it?

One idea triggered the next and was discarded. Rachel, Vijay and Eugen went full speed. The big whiteboard was filling with diagrams and formulae, which showed they were dealing with logic, algorithms, algebra, genetics and other facets of science.

Though the team was on par, just like the hackers in the camp near Berlin, Eugen had become its intellectual leader. When he liked an idea, he called it *bolshoi* – meaning *great* – which turned into a saying as they grew together.

19

Some people possess a rare ability: they can sense numbers and symbols. Numbers have color for some, Eugen heard symbols sound.

One day past midnight, he was sitting alone in front of the clean board, musing. Then he rose and wrote down a long line of mathematical and logical symbols – solemnly and meticulously. Eugen, who cared little for his appearance, cherished calligraphy and the perfect appearance of symbols.

Below this line of symbols he wrote another line, the notes of a fugue, humming its melody while he wrote. Then he stepped back checking the score of symbols and notes and then listening to the harmony of music and theory. He was content, smiled, cleaned the board and went to sleep.

In the morning, the team discussed once again structure, function, interfaces and critical spots of their system's design. Even Rachel – although she did not admit it, was intrigued by the beauty of the architecture, its elegant gestalt.

Finally they could turn to project planning, to an abundance of detail: which partners would come aboard, which tasks be worked on in parallel? How to define the milestones, how the versions?

Rachel volunteered to create the testing environment and test the many hundred modules, integrate them and then test the operational systems – a most challenging task. And they determined their way of communication. They had to be careful since students got a kick out of hacking their professors' computers. So, some things they would do in person, face to face, and not via the net.

When at last they gained an overview of the entire project, its size filled them with awe, its grandeur with impatience. Thanks to the ample resources Bill promised, Eugen felt strong and privileged. Pjotr's diamonds were no match. Finally, he could pursue the goal of his life.

20

Its work done, the team spent the last evening on the veranda. Their hosts were serving Mexican drinks and snacks and Vijay's guitar sounded in the balmy air as he sang *Good Vibrations*. It fit their mood. When he sang the Beach Boys song *Wouldn't It Be Nice,* Rachel joined in, harmonizing in Alto. When Vijay praised Rachel's voice *bolshoi,* they laughed and cheered.

Bill: „O.k., you must have solved the million dollar problem. Now let me hear what it is."

Vijay: „An armada of bots will be combing the net, checking every corner. Pretty intelligent little blood hounds they are …"

Rachel: „… Big Brother will keep an eye on terrorists …"

Eugen: „… something radically new: bots spy and learn, proliferate and adapt …"

Vijay: „… and this happens incredibly fast, exponentially."

Bill rose lifting his glass as if to toast them, but remained skeptical:

„No small potatoes, so it seems. My friends, can you pull this off?"

Bill guessed his remark would hit home. At breakfast he had overheard that they had fought over their risks for the better part of the night. He guessed only Eugen's will and persuasion had made them play and sing again.

Eugen never denied the monstrous, all-too-obvious technical challenge. And he always kept a sober attitude, never spoke of fame and glory. He only insisted they had to take risk, because so much was at stake. They resembled the tiny squad of Spartans defending Greece at a narrow passage between rocks at Thermopylae against the mighty Persian army.

Bill's remark dispelled the good mood bringing their worries back.

Eugen: „We have no choice, Bill. It's all or nothing, make or break."

Rachel shook her head and clenched her fists.

„My god, Eugen, you are pushing your luck, you demand the impossible."

She was utterly alarmed.

„We need a more practical solution, simple and safe, and we need it right now."

Bill, however, didn't want to rush things. Beaten paths and shortcuts wouldn't get him anywhere – this he knew. Even Pjotr had seen that.

Rachel: „Haven't you heard: they hacked the French Institute for Network Security. There are the best. This holy grail of security is better-watched than Fort Knox ever was."

Bill: „Sure, I have heard about the drama."

Rachel: „Drama? It's a disaster, a 9/11. Somewhere out there is a new Lord of the Rings, a Dark Master of the Internet. Bill, we need bots now, on the spot. Have you any idea what is happening in Palestine?"

Bill: „Haste makes waste, Rachel. Don't you forget: the world's intellectual elite will work for us. We have the means."

Bill rose and looked in turn at Vijay, Rachel und Eugen, assessing the team. Was it still on its mission or already broken? He turned to Eugen:

„Do you remember the crypt of Saint Antoine? There you said: a grand idea forms a grand team. Well, you may have a grand idea, but you have to believe in it. All of you."

21

Eugen suspected that Rachel had not yet grasped that bots could backfire in an unimaginable way. She had probably never considered the worst case scenario. Therefore he confronted her.

„Listen: Flawed or sick, malicious bots running loose in the wild – that is my worst nightmare. The world would be overrun by devils and monsters."

They saw Eugen shiver.

Rachel: „But why put everything into the bots at once? Omit introspection, cut out learning functions and all the other luxuries."

Eugen cursed in Russian and countered:

„Cripples won't help us. You know that."

Rachel: „Damned gambler. You always go for the jackpot. You want the perfect creature, you want to be god himself. It's a sin."

After voicing its worst fears, the team was petrified, sitting in silence. Rachel closed her eyes and Eugen stared at the ground. Even the dog lay motionless. At last Rachel rose, looked at Eugen and paused. Her brain followed his arguments while her heart revolted.

Thus caught in a double bind she began to pray in a soft voice: *The Lord is my Shepherd.* Then she stretched and said:

„God bless us."

Rachel had found the right tone and the team relaxed. They looked at each other and knew: in spite of all doubts no one had lost confidence. Vijay put his arms around Eugen's and Rachel's shoulders. Then they formed a circle and cheered when Bill shouted his football team's rallying cry:

„*Gig 'em Aggies.*"

It was the beginning of a grand experiment.

22

Chuck waited for the team in his elegant office offering an impressive view of the capital even now in the rain. Only the American flag, no pictures, decorated the sparsely-furnished room which told visitors: *here resides a level-headed man who is getting ahead.*

The team entered and Chuck greeted it:

„Hi Bill, hi Rachel, good to meet you … and you must be Eugen … and Vijay? Welcome."

They shook hands and sat down around the table. Chuck got down to business right away.

„From now on, you are under contract. I will provide all you need – money and cover. You can reach me at any time – day or night."

He turned to Eugen.

„Here are the essentials – credit cards, cells, passport, driver's license, social security number. And this paper explains our instructions. Read it carefully and then destroy it. Questions? Coffee anyone?"

After this cool introduction they had refreshments and took seats in front of a large screen. A projector showed the blue print of a ship of enormous proportions. And a title read *The Jennifer Project*.

Chuck: „We will watch a film, a Hollywood production. It will teach you the basics of camouflage and deception. You will need it."

In 1968 the revolutionary new Soviet submarine K-129 sank by accident. Moscow knew neither what had happened, nor where the ship lay. It remained missing and a huge loss. Its noiseless propulsion and nuclear intercontinental missiles would have changed the stalemate of strategic weapons in favor of the Soviets – once and for all.

The US sonic surveillance of the Pacific recorded an explosion and, thus, located the boat near Hawaii. A monster – larger and more modern than their own ships rested there in the deep, 5000 meters below surface. It was a treasure, back in Cold War times, when the Vietnam war was raging. And it was a singular chance to surpass the Russians if it was recovered.

Hundreds of experts went to work to build a vessel big enough to lift the submarine from the deep sea, enclose it and bring it to shore. Nothing like it had ever been attempted before. Now it was being done under public scrutiny.

Chuck: „The question is: How could that happen without alarming the world or luring in spies? Watch the movie."

They watched a film that had no happy ending. When lifted, the sub broke apart in the middle and was recovered only in part. And one insider betrayed the endeavor in the end to the Russians. Still, Jennifer paid off.

Chuck: „So, it's clear who built the vessel: a tycoon, one of the super-rich, a maniac, whose passion for women and adventure gave him a mystic aura. And the entire world knew about his latest obsession: to collect manganese nodules from the ocean floor and earn another billion dollars.

Behind this facade operated a tiny team that kept the ship's true mission to itself. "

Eugen began to understand why Bill had never mentioned Chuck. One didn't talk about Chuck to newcomers, let alone Indians and Russians.

I.A. RESEARCH CORP was written at the entrance to the building where they were sitting together. Was I.A. short for International Affairs? It would fit.

Obviously Bill knew Chuck well. One boozy evening at the fireplace, Bill had told them about a satellite project that perhaps reached back in time like the Jennifer Project. Had both projects been international affairs? Chuck's appearance in any case left no doubt: he was the initiator of the Bot Project and its strongman.

Chuck: „My friends, you will start under a less spectacular pretense than Jennifer. I named your project *Cognomorphic Analysis of Internet Security Hazards (CAI)*, a deliberate title leaving you plenty of room. Rachel, it comes with a grant and officially goes to your institute. The contract is here, ready to sign."

Chuck pressed a button and Karen, his assistant entered. Smiling, she stated she was to handle all legal and financial matters of CAI. Then she asked them to sign some papers, wished them well and left, concluding the administrative part of the meeting. Chuck summed up:

„The only ones who know the project's purpose are sitting at this table. And there are only three persons who know how the many components of a bot integrate, who know its architecture. Only three keys to bot-technology exist – your brains."

Bill and Chuck looked at Eugen, Rachel and Vijay. They seemed pleased with their privileges – having all the means and support they could wish for. At last Chuck rose.

„Then we agree. That's good and suffices for today. My friends, find the terror, hunt it down and destroy it. Good luck."

23

„Oh shit, damned shit. We cannot leave it at that. I told you."

Lyudmila shouted. She was exhausted, having spent hours hacking a system. Pjotr grabbed the bottle, put down glasses next to her and joined her.

„It doesn't work?"

„Of course it works. It always does. But not fast enough. You hear me? Intrusion must work faster or we'll blow big orders. Got me?"

She had told him more than once, that they would soon run into a giant roadblock. Ordinary hackers concentrated on modern machines and popular software. Lyudmila, however, had to hack all sorts of old computers. Public services, notably in the east, kept antiquated gear in operation, having neither the funds nor the courage to modernize their fossils. Their budgets covered at best quick fixes and workarounds. They muddled through, thanks to people who made a living by fixing old junk.

With time, Lyudmila could break into any system no matter how old and decrepit. She had been hacking computers for the Secret Service, when she worked – quite productively – as an attaché at the embassy in London.

Now, she feared the future. She would have to penetrate dozens of computers of many makes an models at once. She would not have to search for hidden data – this comforted her. And she would not have to deal with exotic languages like Chinese or the 300 languages of India. That, too, facilitated her job. Her customers would only demand to cripple certain targets.

When it came to computers, sabotage was simpler than espionage. She had simulated the effects of sabotage measures and written dossiers about it. And she knocked out computer networks, knew precisely how to hit the nerves of the net.

If a customer wanted a network to stay down for a week, Lyudmila would sleep well. What haunted her sleep was the speed of action forced on her. Sabotage always had to happen at an ideal point in time. Delay was risky and often intolerable.

However, her own speed and that of her colleagues remained limited. This was due to a phenomenon called *combinatorial explosion*. Too many computer models existed – in too many versions and configurations, too many types and variants of operating systems, security mechanisms and connections. The diversity of her targets was daunting.

„Pjotr, we cannot go on devising mechanisms to penetrate and knock out individual targets. We need mechanisms for many types of target, clever mechanisms which can help themselves if a little problem pops up.

You have to do something. We need Eugen. Fast."

„He disappeared without a trace. All his machines are gone. We checked his apartment, checked the neighborhood, pubs, shops. Nothing.

Pjotr poured Cognac and drank to Lyudmila.

„I cannot imagine that anyone of Eugen's caliber can stay incognito for long. I bet his genius will betray him. He will surface somehow. And then I grab him."

„But if our *dear friends in Kiev* got him first?"

„Then we'll have war."

Lyudmila shook her head and they linked arms.

„Nonsense, Pjotr. Now come with me."

24

CAI ran up to speed within weeks. Rachel steered the course of her institute with an iron hand. Vijay lured his team by promising cutting-edge research that happens once in a lifetime. Eugen, however, was travelling many countries, visiting and testing R&D organizations, scouting for cooperation and entering contracts.

Since well-known players compete in contract research Eugen knew where to go and what to expect when aiming for the best.

He took precautions, avoiding companies which had security clearances. He placed orders in small portions and according to specifications which revealed nothing about a deliverable's use. And he made sure no client knew about any other client. He even kept his itinerary secret. Thus, the NSA wouldn't have a chance to infer the whole from its parts and get wise.

Eugen eventually returned to Grenoble, met Jean at the institute and inquired how the *goodbye-hack* had turned out.

Jean: „You can't imagine if you've never stirred up a hornet's nest. First we had utter confusion, then a stampede and pure panic. At last, the President tried to cover things up.“

„Not a good idea.“

„True, the genie was already out of the bottle. Thus, we had no choice but to dismiss the myth of security and shock the world.“

„Indeed. I read your publication *The Passive Defense of the Internet is Doomed to Fail.* Congratulations – you were brave and clever.“

„My arguments caused quite a stir, provoking politicians and journalists alike. And you won't believe it: Even the hacker scene was in an uproar. They called me a *Slave of the Establishment*. But in the end, I guess, my argument wins.“

Jean had argued convincingly: It is impossible to shield computer networks because they are complex and by necessity flawed. A network's flaws and complexity renders it indefensible.

Jean: „Remember the end of the Middle Ages when walls would no longer save the castles. Troops were the best defense. Troops were able to strike first and fast in case of threat, and attack in order to defend. Today's networks are like castles and, therefore, doomed. Thus I argued for high-tech troops.

„When I read your paper, I couldn't believe my eyes. You argued for attack in a society which has settled for defense. How did you survive?"

„Ha. Feelings ran high in a storm of protest. Some talked of a new Cold War, of Nazi methods and of public terror. One newspaper ran the headline: *Terror & Counterterror: Internet War Brewing*."

„I am sorry, Jean, you must have gone through hell."

„But I also had fun. I laughed about a German lady who accused me of blasphemy – of betraying the holy freedom of the Internet. She wished for the inquisition to cure heretics like me."

Of course, thousands had showered Jean with applause: finally someone had the guts to tell the unadorned truth: that hackers will kill the net and democracy, and that all free men must bite back.

Jean: „By the way, Sophie wants to see uncle Eugen. She loves your matryoshka and calls it *Mohsa*."

„I promise to see my little friend. But I came because Odile's research intrigues me. Please tell her I arrived."

Jean signaled his colleague.

Eugen: „Good to meet you again, professor."

„Non non non – just call me Odile. You are interested in our parsers?"

„That's why I am here for and for your scanners of Oriental scripts."

„Ah bon. Please come with me."

Both disappeared in the institute's inner sanctum, behind double doors secured by eye-scanners.

25

On a cold winter evening Jean dropped Eugen off at Anna's house. She bid him welcome and lead him past the fragrant kitchen to the parlor where a fire was burning and the table laid. Eugen was touched by the warm and cultivated atmosphere of the room. Anna poured him a glass.

„Spend the time with a Pastis, Eugen, dinner is almost ready."

Eugen studied Anna's library scanning books in foreign languages – Greek, Latin, and Arabic, written by Aristotle, Thomas Aquinas, Averroes and Avicenna. He read names of little import for Soviet education, but great names no doubt.

He took an open book from Anna's desk and put it beside the dining table. Anna would, as always, serve delicious food, the wine would taste great and they would have a lively conversation. Here, Eugen missed St. Petersburg less than ever.

Anna served *pieds paquets*, a Provençale specialty. Sheep's feet, filled with tripe, garlic and herbs cooked the whole day in red wine – not exactly Haute Cuisine, but unsurpassed on a winter evening. Anna put the earthen pot on the table.

Eugen was carried away by the strong flavor of the dish and showed it while devouring the meat and piling up bones, while uttering Russian sounds of pleasure.

Anna smiled, pleased. She believed in the dishes of the poor people, if they were prepared with love and the herbs of the garden. At last, Eugen pointed to the book on the table.

„Anna, what makes philosophy interesting? What is it your students want to know? What are you working on?"

„This book, here, deals with freedom, the free will of man – a hot topic since the times of Aristotle. My students say, the topic is sexy. Others say there is no such thing as a free will, because our brains don't allow us to always control our decisions. They maintain, things can happen in our brain just like that and we can do nothing about it. That's crazy, isn't it?"

Eugen: „I only know that my bots are free. No one can force them. They do what they deem important. Always."

„Really? Let's move over to the fireplace."

They sat down in armchairs in front of the fireplace.

Eugen: „My bots learn whatever they want to learn. And they stay wherever they choose to stay – in Russia, Arabia or here, in France. They live in a world without boundaries. Believe me, that's why I envy my bots."

Anna seemed impressed, put wood on the fire, grasped her glass and leaned back.

„I take it they also have a sense of beauty?"

Eugen sighed. Anna had touched on a sore spot.

„A bot only lives in a world of bits and bytes."

Eugen lifted his glass and viewed the color of the wine, lit by the fire.

„This delicacy means nothing to him. Still worse, when I play Bach: he can hear it, store and analyze it. But to love Bach's music the way I love it – that he can't."

„And it grieves you?"

„If I could change it, I would give my right hand."

„Then, unfortunately, your bot will never be able to tell good from bad."

Eugen pondered in silence. Good and bad? These biblical categories didn't crop up in the domain of algorithms, inferences and knowledge bases.

„So what? A bot will be a marvel nonetheless, will amaze professionals and horrify villains."

„Perhaps it will. But bear in mind, the good and the beautiful belong together. You cannot have one without the other. Greek philosophers called it *kalós kai agathós*. How free can a bot be who doesn't know beauty? Will he have the freedom to do good?"

Now both looked at the fire, lost in thought. Eugen murmured *kalós kai agathós*.

„Anna, do you believe in this old stuff?"

„Yes, my friend. This stuff has not been refuted in 2000 years. And your technology is not going to change that either."

As the fire burnt down, Anna thought of her student' pains in finding their way in a world of great minds. Eugen, too, would need time.

„Eugen, please play piano for me."

He longed to play for her and thank her for the wonderful evening.

„Please name a number."

„Five."

Soon the clear harmonies of the Brandenburg Concerto No. 5 filled the house.

26

While driving from the camp down south to the Drôme Jean had talked about his home, where Eugen should feel comfortable and perhaps take root.

Jean: „I was born with wanderlust, always longing for the far away. Many times I hitchhiked through Spain down into Morocco – was addicted to the road, drugged by making mileage, finding rest only in one particular spot: Marrakech's Jema el Fna, the Place of the Beheaded. After midnight it was bustling with life – Bedouins from the far mountains, storytellers, fortune tellers, snake charmers, kebab cooks and bands playing through the night on instruments I had never seen before."

Eugen was moved, turned his ring and nodded.

„Hm. Marrakech might have been like Bukhara a hundred years ago, when the Silk Road was still the greatest road on earth."

Jean could not make sense of this cryptic remark. Apparently it was full of unspoken memories. So, he went on.

"Even more exotic were leftists – hip and young and far out. I always wanted to understand their excitement for Marx and Mao's Bible, but never got down to the nitty-gritty. What is it?"

„I could teach you Marxism for a whole semester, if you like, but I could not inspire you. Anyone who, as you say, loves Marrakech, Bunuel and Django Reinhardt, that is, Surrealism and Jazz, is entirely lost for the great Proletarian Revolution.

By the way, you told me a lot about your mother. What about your father?"

"He lives in America. Anna got to know and love him after she went to Paris for her first job at the Sorbonne. And then I arrived."

"That, probably, wasn't easy for her."

"Our family backed us up. It is a great family. At a wedding, all the women cook and bake and a hundred people celebrate. You'll see."

The family endured hard times. Anna's father had to hide from the Nazis after joining the Resistance and fighting in the Vercors. He survived one year living in the woods. He was clever, but without his family he would have starved.

27

Stanford University, named after its founder, a western railroad magnate, differs from the elite universities of the east. Their dignified architectures, lawns and ivy-covered walls remind of their English models, while around Stanford, as the university is dubbed, Spanish names prevail for towns and roads, like *El Camino Real*. The Stanford campus impresses with southwestern flair and many cherish it as the cradle of Silicon Valley and its prime source of ideas. Little wonder, it attracts the student elites of the world.

Eugen chose this exceptional place to spend a sabbatical and concentrate on the development of his bots, which had reached a critical phase. Soon it would become evident whether bots achieved what they were supposed to.

Eugen had travelled many countries, found software talent, placed orders and spent much money. The results flowed back to Rachel's institute, where bot-version 0.5 was up and running. If it had been a human being, doctors would attest it a stable constitution, faultless vital function and sound senses. Still, nothing could be said about its character, self-awareness, determination and potential for development.

After flying in from Boston, Eugen was sitting in Vijay's white convertible, a vintage Alfa Romeo. Its well-tended coating and leather seats told the connoisseur: *this car is owned by an enthusiast of style*.

An hour ago, cold fog had come up from the ocean across the Coastal Range as on every morning. Now the California sun had burned it away, again creating a sunny, warm winter day. They approached the campus, drove through its palm groves, passed barefoot students playing Frisbee, parked and walked to the main cafeteria.

Hordes of students were underway at noon on bikes, roller skates and rollerblades, jogging, in jeans and shorts. Eugen observed this demonstration of the Californian way of life: everyone seemed relaxed, fit and goal-oriented.

Eugen: „That's the place to be."

„Quite so, my friend. Stanford rocks", Vijay said pointing to a worker who repaired cracks in a wall, „Scaffolds here and there remind you that at Stanford even the earth rocks now and then."

While they were heading for lunch, Eugen reported on Rachel's bot which he had scrutinized the days before:

„It's still a torso, but taking shape. Orientation within the Internet already works fine. The beast masters this maze, always finding its way. And it understands a number of languages – not perfectly, but well enough. Now we can begin to refine the interface between language and cognition – between the system of words and the system of concepts. Introspection, of course, Rachel hasn't even touched on yet. It will be a real brainteaser.

And I must not forget the planning function. Professor Hewitt, once Rachel's mentor, would love it. His *Planner* achieved a breakthrough – back in the seventies."

Newspapers were on display at the bookstore. Eugen stopped to make Vijay aware of the headline *Tel Aviv Endangered.*

„Tel Aviv. This is where Rachel has family, mother and sister. She wanted me to know this."

They went to the cafeteria for a snack.

Vijay: „Next time we'll visit the faculty club. But here is where Stanford's heart beats. If you care for yoghurt, juice or salad, this is the right place. Here people are food cognizant."

The young people at the next table – all of them of Asian descent – observed the odd couple. Vijay wore black trousers with creases, an embroidered white linen shirt, rimless spectacles, elegant shoes and a gold chain. Eugen, who looked down and out in Alexandrovsky Park, wore new clothes but still neglected fashion. His drab outfit seemed to say: *don't be sidetracked by my appearance – behold my intellectual excellence.*

On their way back they discussed the progress made by Rachel at MIT but soon talked about Rachel's disposition and management style.

Vijay: „Have you heard? Her staff calls her *the whip*."

„Little wonder. She seems driven by nervous energy. But why this haste?"

„Remember the last day on the ranch? She feared a *Dark Lord of the Internet* and urged us to use bots on the spot."

„Yes, I could sense her fear."

„Does she know something we don't know?"

„Possibly. After all she is a member of the Council of National Security."

At the institute, Vijay opened the door to Eugen's new domain, the office of a retired professor. Publications on Molecular Biology filled the bookshelves, covering an entire wall. Dark paneling on the others walls served as background for framed paintings. Photos, certificates and awards gave evidence of a long academic career. Heavy furniture, leather armchairs and a couch, rugs and a spacious desk of reddish wood were relics of bygone times.

Eugen looked out of the window and saw the lawn and a bush covered with buds.

Vijay: „It will blossom all blue in spring."

„Charming, my friend, I am glad you invited me here."

Then he inspected the computers, booted them and was content. They were the special devices he had ordered. Nothing was missing, he could begin.

28

Eugen crossed the hall, passed a bulletin board and a poster inviting to the International Conference of Mathematical Genetics and Genetic Algorithms, in Shanghai China, and entered Vijay's office. A desk of acrylic glass stood beteen white walls, one chair in front, and two chairs behind. A file cabinet stood centered on the side wall, to the left of it a guitar, to its right a futon, a Buddha figure on top.

Screen, mouse and keyboard were on the desk and a stylized double-helix. *Award, Computational Genetics, Vijay Chandra Yunus* were engraved at the bottom.

This minimalist ambience inspired to meditation, but Eugen immediately turned to the screen where Vijay showed some bizarre things: colorful incunabula, codices, and ancient, illustrated handwritings in Latin, Gothic, Greek, Arabic and Persian. Most documents had suffered in the course of centuries, yet looked fascinating. Eugen was glued to the screen.

Vijay: "You are looking into the digital archive of the Library of Congress. And you are looking at bots in disguise."

But Eugen could not recognize them.

„These images look like originals, but they aren't. They are studded with bot-code. Look here."

Vijay showed two identical-looking images of a medieval prayer book – a blooming garden in the foreground of a castle, trees and mountains in the background and saints crowding the blue sky above.

„Left, the original right, the copy – subtly altered in color, form and texture. Like a water-mark, the alterations are very difficult to discern, I admit. They hold the information. Imagine, one in a hundred pixels contains a bit of code. Tell me: isn't the bot-disguise cute?"

After Eugen compared the images, Vijay started the film *Some Like it Hot*, showing a great scene: Marilyn Monroe gracefully tripping on high heels along the train to Florida, followed by the *ladies* Jack Lemmon und Tony Curtis, imitating her exciting walk.

„This is my version of the film, as you might have guessed. But not bad, is it? It contains the entire software of Rachel's bot.

„Bolshoi, my friend, you are going to win the Turing Prize."

„Don't make me too proud, else I'll be reborn a bot."

They laughed and knew they had taken an important hurdle. The Internet stored images and videos galore – hideouts for armies of bots. But Eugen addressed one problem.

„The entire code in one film – in one location?"

„No. The code will be distributed, as we decided on the ranch. Look what my post graduates built. Here is a bot in action."

Eugen observed a strange spectacle as the screen came alive. It seemed as if a giant swarm of glassy bees had landed in the branches of an imaginary tree. Its wafting gestalt was composed of transparent parts. Eugen looked through them, deep into a structure of boundless complexity. Parts of the bot pulsed, changing colors from the greyish hues of glass to transparent red.

The swarm resembled an imperfect sphere with missing parts at the surface and deep down. Then the shape changed into the form of a skull, where parts of the brain reddened and then paled again. Eugen looked at the dynamic software of an active bot and thought: *bolshoi, this guy lives.*

„Look how it is shedding useless parts and gathering new ones from the Internet. No bot is ever completely in one place. I guess that's what you wanted."

Whenever a new module attached, it extended connectors like tentacles – reaching into the structure, searching for partners. When the newcomer's handshake failed, the module flashed up and fell down with a crunching sound.

„Watch out now, the show will soon be over."

A part of the bot deep down began to glow – and then seemed to disintegrate. Then it darkened, became blackish and seemed to paralyze its environment. All reddish parts paled and hundreds of parts dropped off with a deep sigh. Only a thin, grid-like structure remained, shaped like the bones of a skull.

Eugen: „It seems the beast suffered an infarction. What happened?"

„Apparently it's the Introspector. It works well in Meta 1 and moves on to Meta 2. As I understand it, it starts to control the behavior of the bot and then controls its own behavior. But it never returns from Meta 2. It grabs all the resources it can get – devours storage space as if in panic. And eventually it is over. That's all I know. Good that you are here now."

„I expected a problem like that, but it must wait. You must get along without me. I'll be traveling for a while."

29

Asians, Africans and Europeans worked in the lab in Istanbul, which Eugen visited. It was one of the modern centers of contract research of the upcoming city. He had visited similar labs in Astana, Chennai und Singapore. Now he studied the screen while Shika explained the state of work:

„The language system will soon be complete. Urdu and Arabic are finished. I am testing Bangla – visual & audio."

Snippets of text – handwriting and print - appeared in rapid sequence. A line showed the English translation in parallel, scrolling over the screen like a ticker text.

Below, boxes indicated the software components involved in the translation process. Their oscillating size and color reflected the states of activation: routine work, problem handling, success or failure.

„Here are the statistics. The rate of recognition is 97%. I am proud. Now the audio function."

After Shika und Eugen put on headsets, they heard fragments of speech, spoken and sung by high and low male and female voices. Then Shika turned it off and explained the statistics.

„Hit rate 53%. That's good, given the often bad acoustics and the many dialects. But we recognize important keywords with a probability of 89%. I guess we did it."

„You did a great job. Be proud of it. I thank you."

Eugen shook hands with Shika and her colleagues and bade them farewell. Again he thought of the ambivalent nature of the Internet, this hotbed of surveillance, porn and crime, as Jean called it. But it had also turned into a hotbed of innovation, had advanced speech processing and automatic translation with unbelievable power. He remembered when these technologies were still cutting edge research. Now they were available for little money in computer games, browsers and cars. And he was benefitting – his bots would understand what they read. Now he could tackle the next challenges which would be much more difficult.

30

Eugen was hurrying in anticipation to his last station, Betty and Joe. For months he had tried to find such battle-hardened science cracks, but without avail: their heydays were long past. Luckily Bill had remembered Betty, who once helped his project survive a critical situation. A satellite was to be launched shortly but before it did, his team had to fix one last flaw hiding in the dozens of interconnected computers of the satellite. No testing software made transparent what was really going on inside this little network. Except for Betty's novel testing gear, which had left the team in awe.

Joe had been one of those fabulous *compulsive programmers*, who slept on cots in computer centers, to use every second of computer time, then the scarcest resource.

Later, the upcoming cosmology excited him and he got hooked on the question of *how galaxies evolve*. Joe simulated such distributed dynamic systems of a million stars and impressed the expert world. Later he took to less celestial objects, visualizing whatever television and the movies required – swarms, flocks, hordes and herds of products or actors.

Betty had lived through all the ups and downs of Artificial Intelligence. In fact, she was part of the system which produced romantic hopes of achievement and ludicrous promises. In the end she failed miserably in taking the highest hurdle: *complexity*. Intelligent systems proved adventurously complex.

Ironically, she failed while trying to simplify matters. Her *Architecture for Knowledge Integration* had made her famous. It offered all known tools used to represent knowledge: logical calculi, neural networks, ontologies, concepts and objects, as well as programming languages like Lisp. Knowledge engineers would be able to represent expert knowledge in whatever form they deemed best.

Today, nobody gives a damn for her brilliant, but overly ambitious approach. Eugen did not care for it either, but deemed Betty's experience invaluable.

31

From the airport, Eugen drove through the endless suburbs of Los Angeles into the hills bordering the desert, parked at a heavily guarded entrance and was frisked. He entered an empty room, put his briefcase on a table, left the building by the rear exit, and drove a car without a license plate to a run-down building in a remote part of the campus. The image of a skunk was pinned to the door and the words *Skunk Works III* named the place. Here, sparse bureaucracy, extreme challenges and personal freedom attracted creative minds.

Betty and Joe were immersed in work as he entered. Computers seemed to mushroom in the messy place, leaving little room for a fridge and a fan, the only luxury items. A large poster showed *Sky and Water*, the famous drawing by the logician M.C. Escher: a fish in deep water morphs step by step into a bird, emerges from the water and takes to the skies.

But it is not only the fish which evolves, it's also its environment – initially water then air – which turns into a bird and lets the fish vanish.

How strange, Eugen wondered looking at the large letters below the poster, heralding Betty's credo: *Evolution is not a free lunch.*

Betty didn't greet Eugen but involved him at once.

„Hey, come here and look at this crap."

Eugen felt like being in the Chaos Camp once more. He and Betty stared at a screen where strange creatures were popping up, displaying bizarre organs and extremities. They resembled totally artificial insects, viruses, jellyfish and silly toys. Eugen thought: *It's a Carnival of Structures.*

„Joe had an idea and I can use it. It's awesome", Betty said.

Years ago Joe had rendered a film scene where an army of robots defends the human race from an attack by aliens. He used the skeletons of these robots again to visualize the structure of bot-software. An observer would see fins, legs, tails, antlers and tentacles, each of which had a special meaning.

„I'll turn these carcasses into real beasts with skin and hair and scales as soon as we got a grip on your stuff. What great shit it is. I am pissed."

Betty explained the wrench in the works. The software *Goaler, Planer, Motivator* usually worked out nicely. But she called it *Bermuda Triangle* because the bot got lost in it sporadically for unknown reasons. It entered the triangle but never exited again. She suspected the Motivator to be the culprit and spent night after night tinkering with it until she gave up.

„At the slightest change this beast goes bonkers. I tried to discard it entirely, but didn't succeed."

The Motivator allocates resources like rights and budgets to functional components. One component may need the right to access secure data, another a budget to use a decryption service. Only if enabled, i.e. motivated, the function can do anything.

Eugen pitied Betty:

„True, the Motivator is a tricky beast, because it has to know so much about past attempts, current undertakings and pending jobs."

„Yes of course, but that's not the issue. Eugen, I hate you for your cryptic programming style. A few more comments wouldn't have hurt."

„Oh, I am terribly sorry, Betty. I guess I have been trained to keep ideas undercover – back in the USSR."

„It gets even better. What really drives me mad is the learning function you built into the Motivator. It is truly diabolic. Okay, okay, I know it makes the motivator smarter, but it also alters it continually. If I understand this damned beast today, I know it will tick differently tomorrow.

Eugen, I fumed and cursed you. And then Joe tried to save me."

Joe recommended what he called *final coup*, his last resort when cornered:

„When I am stuck for good, I just guess, relying on my gut feeling. So I told Betty to change the bot at random and see what happens and then make an even better change."

„Bill, Joe excels at guessing. I envy him, when he mixes the best cocktails from a few ingredients at hand. But his trick doesn't work for me."

Betty sighed. The number of ways to change a bot was staggering; millions and millions. Yet she continued to fumble and Joe's software visualized what happened.

„Look, one tentacle shrunk, but grew a new fork. That's because I shortened a loop by inserting another exit. Perhaps the bot got stuck in this loop before. Let's see what it will do now."

Shortly after, the beast with the forked tentacle flashed in red and disappeared, as if swallowed by the Bermuda Triangle. New creatures appeared on screen, were tested and disappeared.

Eugen watched Betty wrestling with a tough problem, one she might never solve. After a little while Betty switched the screen off, turning to Eugen.

„Joe has helped me a lot. No, I have neither charted nor fathomed the Bermuda Triangle. I don't really understand the problem, but I got a feeling. And it's a bad feeling, Eugen. We may be trapped in a strange loop. If that's the case, so help us god."

„Poor Betty, I can't help you now, I have to catch a plane. But please carry on. I need you and I trust you."

Then he pointed at the poster on the wall. Its subtitle read like a bad omen.

„You knew it: Evolution is not a free lunch."

Joe: „Right. And we will lose this damned game. I'd bet my life on it."

„No bets this time, Joe. The whole project is at stake. I must leave you now. Thanks my friends that you are still playing along."

Eugen embraced Betty. When he went with Joe to the door, Betty yelled after them:

„Just get out of my way, you geezers. All this damned bot needs is female intelligence."

32

One night, Vijay came to see Eugen in his office.

„Still fiddling with your darlings?"

„No. I got mail."

„Ah, from that fabulous French lady?"

„Mail from my bot. Come here and take a look."

Below the heading *Protrepticos* several pages followed filled with Greek letters. The message closed with the word *beautiful*.

„What the heck does it mean?"

„I have no idea. I guess he is testing my wits. Sends me weird stuff and always adds *beautiful*. And I can never figure out what it means. I only know he is much smarter than I am."

„Nonsense, you are talking nonsense. He is only a bot."

„No. This bot is the first of a new generation. A major breakthrough, I assume. For months I have been fiddling with his architecture."

The concept *Society of Mind,* invented by the old wizard nicknamed *Marvelous Minsky*, inspired Eugen. It convinced him the brain worked like a society of peers

– there were no chiefs, only Indians. The brain was populated by specialists and every one of them connected to all the others. These connections made the difference – what a difference.

Consequently, Eugen re-designed bots from scratch, replacing control hierarchies with a kind of bourse. At a stock market, brokers shout and signal and all can see the latest state of affairs. At the bot's bourse all software functions exchange insights and opinions, plans and decisions. This bourse serves as a universal connector.

„Vijay, it is a quantum leap."

„Wow. When did you do it?"

„While travelling. I spent fascinating nights in boring hotels, if you can believe me."

„You flattened hierarchies. I am fascinated by flat structures. Ants, algae, cells, fish and birds; plants prefer them. Unfortunately, they are no panacea. Every herd of cattle and every pack of wolves has a leader."

Eugen looked in admiration at Vijay who spotted the weak point immediately:

„I am sadly aware of it. The *Society of Mind* must implement self-control – thus a kind of leader. What a pity. Flat structures are so beautiful."

They discussed the bourse-concept and in the end assumed the pros outweighed the cons by far.

Eugen: „Then it's decided. We'll switch to the new bots. The old bots, which Rachel is testing now, are garbage."

„Watch out. Testing the new bots means weeks and weeks of work for her. Rachel is already counting the days until bot-launch – when she can pull the trigger. Eugen, she will throw a fit and give you hell."

„Of course she will kill me, but she will treat you much more gently, young man. So, please do me a favor my friend. Go and break the news to her."

This was bad news for Vijay as he feared the trip to see Rachel. How could he possibly sell her on the new architecture?

Vijay: „I guess, the new bot is much less complex and thus much more reliable. Correct?"

„Well, we might be in for a surprise. Betty is having a rough time right now. "

When they were about to leave, Vijay had a last look on the message titled Protrepticos. It looked rather outlandish.

„Wait. Tell me, where is this bot?"

„Here today, gone tomorrow. I only know he loves to hang around in libraries."

„He is free?"

„You bet. Free to read, learn and move."

An immature bot in freedom? Wasn't this the worst case to happen? But Eugen smiled.

„Don't worry, I deactivated the replicator. He cannot proliferate, remains a singleton forever."

Why had Eugen done that? On the way to the parking lot, Eugen put his arm around Vijay's shoulders and – for the first time – spoke about his feelings.

„It feels like magic, to free a young bot. Thinking of it is still gives me goosebumps. I see the young falcon on the rim of the aerie, finally spreading its wings and floating into the wide world. You see, it's a sentimental story.

I am overjoyed when he visits me every once in a while. And I love his messages, even though I can't understand them. They tell me he's alive."

33

Rachel left the taxi, entered the Israeli embassy and was escorted to an office where an elderly man greeted her and regarded her intently.

Rachel: „Thanks, Ambassador, for receiving me so promptly."

„My pleasure. After all, you are a member of the Security Council. "

Rachel asked to get to the core of the matter at once.

„A new kind of cruise missile has been developed in the Far East, much more advanced than Kassam rockets. Eleven of them are underway to Dubai onboard the vessel Rho Bao Ra. They are about to land in four days. Then they will be smuggled into Lebanon."

The ambassador took notes and again looked at Rachel.

„Amazing. How did you obtain the information?"

„This I can't tell you Ambassador, but you should know that only I can access a source which is absolutely reliable."

Again, the ambassador studied his counterpart, then sat next to Rachel, seized her wrist, loosened the bracelet and touched the symbols on it.

Rachel: „This charm belonged to my grandmother. Ambassador, what are you going to do?"

„This, professor, I cannot tell you, but you should know, I won't stay idle."

He gave the bracelet back and, on parting, blessed his visitor in Yiddish:

„Maseltow, Rachele, Hazloche un Broche."

34

Massive old buildings as well as super-modern architecture shape the campus of the Massachusetts Institute of Technology, MIT. Dignified portals above a flight of stairs stand next to facades without a single horizontal or vertical plane, seemingly created at the spur of the moment.

This was Rachel's realm, where she configured and tested bots. The testing ground had grown to enormous proportions and diversity, incorporating most computer types used in the Internet as well as clones and mirrors of applications from numerous countries. Companies rented this mini-Internet to test novel network technology. Here, bots were tested while staying in quarantine, out of the Internet.

Back from the excursion to the embassy and on the way to her office, Rachel opened a camera- and sensor-controlled door. The room behind was filled with racks of servers and a tangle of cables. Fans and air conditioning were humming monotonously in dim lighting. Diagrams were on display on a long row of screens. They made the woman who tended the big machine look like a physician in an ICU.

„Hi, Debbie."

The network manager watched her with concern:

„You look terrible."

„I know. Lack of sleep, time's running out. But to major matters: did you complete the net?"

„The Japanese stuff arrived this week. Finally. It's the rest of the gear that controls production plants and factories. I'll have it installed this weekend and then I am done."

„Sorry Debbie, it must wait. Vijay will deliver a new version on Friday. He said they tinkered with the core. So, a whole test-run is due.

I bet we owe this to another quirk of Eugen. How I hate this maniac. He is shooting for the moon."

„What do you mean? He is too ambitious?"

„I can't read this guy at all – never met anyone like him. For one, he is only going for the jackpot but, on the other hand, he wants to make dead sure his game works out. He is a bull and a chicken at the same time.

Debbie, my problem is, I am not playing in his league. He is way beyond me."

35

Vijay entered Rachel's office. It looked like a tedious place in spite of a couch and a few cheerful paintings by her children. He greeted her fleetingly, putting a memory stick on her desk

„Here is version 7. You were dying to get it, were you not?"

„Bullshit. You are wasting time, once again. Version 6 was perfect."

„No, not perfect, the new version is a lot safer. And version 8 is coming up."

„Gods, going at this speed will cost us another year."

„Version 6 could cost us a lot more."

„How can you say that? You damned perfectionists are driving me mad. Look at this."

She started a recording of a newscast showing hooded men, explosions and destruction.

„It happened yesterday in Lebanon."

Agitated, she switched off the video.

„Terror is having a breakthrough. It is at our doorstep. Wake up Stanford. You hear me?"

Then she calmed down and turned to Vijay. He picked up the stick and presented it on his palm like a treasure.

„Don't you forget version 7. And don't you forget your risks. Listen. It only needs one single flaw and your bots confuse friend with foe. What if they turn against us? Havoc as never before. Worse: nothing could stop them. Think of it."

Rachel suddenly turned pale, dropped into a seat, clasped her belly, groaned and deflated.

In an instant, Vijay was at her side, put her legs up, covered her with his jacket and held her cold, quivering hand. No doubt, Rachel went beyond her limits pushing the work on bots. Vijay saw exhaustion in her face and felt her angst. What had happened? Would she talk?

But Rachel didn't want to talk as she slowly recovered, forcing herself to stand up.

„Sorry Vijay. Debbie is waiting. Let's go."

36

Eugen pushed the plate with the rest of his meal aside, making room for the sketch he was brooding on. He did not notice the pleasant ambience of the faculty club, the trees and flowers, nor did he greet the friendly nodding colleagues passing the table. He did notice that his thoughts were stuck and he had no idea what would help him on.

Thus he decided for a *Walk with Bach*, a brain-stimulating walk while listening to the Italian Concerto. This combination of sports and music had helped him often. He put on earphones, let the iPod play, and went back to his office.

As he entered, he heard the last sounds of the concert, then turned to the screen and was appalled. From afar it looked like screaming discord. He murmured:

„How ugly he is. Now I see it. Bach opened my eyes.“

The screen was cluttered by a 3D-representation of the bot and many small windows. Each of them was linked to a certain spot in the bot's brain and showed what was going on inside – streams of symbols, oscillating curves or alarms. The scene resembled an operating room. Most probes – the windows – were alive; no doubt the Introspector was working. But had it advanced?

Eugen zoomed into one of the probes and observed the sluggish flow of hexadecimal numbers at in interface. When the flow stopped, he was certain the Introspector had failed again. Old Joe was right after all.

Groaning, Eugen dropped on the couch talking to himself:

„He won't come back. It is strange. Meta has no boundaries, no horizon. Is like a Riemann Surface: always leading back to itself, having neither beginning nor end. It's the route of the eternal wanderer.“

Then he cursed in Russian and, thus relieved, fell asleep. Eugen spent days in solitude, doggedly fighting the problem he assumed to be a flaw of software architecture and, thus, resolvable. As all attempts failed, it dawned on him: he had misjudged the root of the problem and, therefore, could not apply his axe.

One night at Vijay's, he dropped into a seat, bleary-eyed, crinkled, and unshaven. Vijay teased him:

„My friend, you look like a scruffy bot."

„Listen to me."

When Vijay sensed how troubled Eugen was, he served him a drink, closed the door, sat down on the floor and listened. Eugen began vaguely:

„I gave them consciousness and a sharp mind. My masterpiece."

Vijay saw the face of a beaten man who was suffering. Then it broke out of him:

„I cannot control them. Not entirely. Not all of them. Not millions. Nobody can. Vijay they will terrorize us. It's only a matter of time."

He lay down on the floor staring at the ceiling. Then he screamed in Russian before calming down again.

„The Introspector should have done it. But wrong, wrong, wrong!

I pushed too far, overdid complexity. Crossed the line. I am an idiot, only the sorcerer's apprentice."

Eugen paused, sitting still, eyes closed. Then he sighed:

„My game is over. Vijay play guitar for me."

Vijay reached for the guitar, played the tenor voice of a cantata and sang for his guest who did not move. When he finished, Eugen rose, staggered to the door babbling *Anna ...old wisdom ...kalós kai agathós* and left the room.

37

Eugen's office was in a state of chaos: the windows were shaded and the lights burning and illuminating the trash on desk and floor – bottles, cartons, cans, leftovers of food, paper and clothes. The bot shone from the screen – unaltered in its form but the colors had paled and some structures crumbled. Merely one probe displayed a message from time to time, like a feeble pulse.

Vijay found Eugen lying on the couch, looking confused. Obviously he had not showered for days nor changed his clothes. He looked miserable, eyes staring into the distance, lips moving soundlessly, his thoughts cycling forever.

„Eugen!"

Vijay shook his colleague.

„You can't go on like this."

Some rough Russian words followed.

„Get up. Now. Move."

Eugen sat up groaning.

„Need coffee."

Vijay grabbed Eugen under the arms.

„No, my friend, what you need is a doctor. You come with me. Now. Go!"

He pushed Eugen out the door.

38

When Bill arrived at Stanford, Vijay greeted him with relief. They inspected Eugen's office, saw the dirt and the tortured creature on the screen. The room looked more pleasant after the screen was switched off. If this room were an image of the project, it looked bad.

Bill had conferred with Rachel, who had given him hope. She mocked the gadgets made at Stanford, called Eugen *reckless* and pleaded that the bots be launched immediately.

Betty, however, voiced a different opinion. Yes, the bots were almost completed, but not entirely. Bill should remember his old project – when the launch of the satellite failed – and keep the bots locked away.

What now? The ladies contradicted each other, although he trusted both of them. And he remembered that Vijay once remarked the bots were not good enough. Now, Bill questioned him.

„What did you mean?"

„Oh, the bots are extremely clever, no doubt. Never before has anything like them existed. Eugen worked wonders."

„Rachel would support your point of view."

„Just wait. Bots are clever, Bill, clever but not wise. They are merely mercenaries, mere machines. They analyze their environment, but don't sense it. Bill, they are not grounded in life. This flaw will hamper them forever. There is nothing we can do about it."

During the stroll to the Faculty Club for lunch, Bill tried to make sense of Vijay's phrase *grounded in life* which seemed fundamental. Vijay told him that bots were incapable of experiencing life, not even an artificial form of life. Bots did not love, compete and suffer. They were leading an empty life. And Vijay told him, that later on he wanted to research artificial life which was grounded and, thus, made sense.

Bill, who knew little about Vijay, was amazed and alerted. If Eugen dropped out, Vijay had to play a bigger role. But what sort of person was this young Indian who had stayed in the background at the ranch and ever since?

„You didn't seem particularly happy at the ranch. Did the bickering of Rachel and Eugen turn you off?"

„I was fine. Didn't I play and sing on the last evening?"

„Yes, you did. And before?"

„That's a long story."

Vijay told Bill, that he had felt like someone who has just fallen in love but soon after met a still more attractive girl. He was in love with his research of very particular organic structures. He pursued an idea which was his idea alone. And then he was faced with this fantastic idea of bots.

Should he give up his first love for another? This dilemma plagued him until he realized he could have both. Then he had grabbed the guitar and sung.

Structures had fascinated him from childhood on. He had been born in a middle-Indian town, a Buddhist enclave, surrounded by Hindus. Only here, in the diaspora, remained the ancient Buddhist teachings unaltered, handed down from one generation to the next. Here Vijay learned about the elementary structures of circles and trees – the circle of life reborn and the tree of seed and offspring.

Vijay first turned to biology, then to the structures of genes. One assumption turned him on: that intelligence had a structure of its own. He hoped this structure would reveal itself in the brains of humans, mammals and vertebrates, perhaps even in mollusks like the intelligent calamar. But he discovered nothing of the kind. He seemed to hunt a phantom.

Then Eugen opened his eyes: bots had to be intelligent and had to have a structure of their own – a software architecture. Vijay took it as a godsend: Bot intelligence might help him understand biological intelligence after all.

39

During lunch they talked about their boyhood. Bill had experienced the hard free life on the farm of his parents, Vijay the iron rules of his family.

„All my forefathers strove for enlightenment – the well-balanced practice of mind, heart and hands. They called it *order*."

„Does it hold for you, too?

„I value order just like them. I call it *harmony* and I call it *god*."

„It seems to me there is little room for bots in your orderly world."

Vijay put knife and fork down in amazement. Bill seemed to have X-rayed him, read his most private thoughts.

„I am terrified when I look to the future. At this very moment, bots could create havoc, worse than in my worst nightmares."

„Betty told me she discovered a strange structure, an endless loop. She called it *mental prison*. Is this what you are worrying about?"

„Worse, much worse – in a few years, the military will capture bot technology and soon after it will leak to the bad guys, the terrorists."

Vijay was not worried about immature bots getting out of hand, he was worried about mature bots getting into the wrong hands:

„It's unavoidable. And I will be responsible. And you too, Bill."

Slowly, Bill began to understand: the project's success was no longer determined by the scientific talent of Eugen, Rachel and Vijay, but by their inner motives. Back at the ranch he could not have guessed the diverse nature of these driving forces. Only now, in crisis, it became clear and he worried.

40

Eugen, now a patient in a clinic, was sitting in a shady garden. Well dressed, he appeared rested and relaxed. Medication had helped. After a visit to the library, he leafed through a book by the architect Jan Kaplicky, leisurely savoring the aesthetics of the photographs. He saw a shark, a motorcycle, a stingray, sunglasses, a mountain pass, pebbles and water. And he read Kaplicky's brief and cryptic comments such as: *Beauty Understood by Few* or *Color, Coolness, Translucency and much more*.

How strange, Eugen thought, last week these images would have been silent, but now I can hear their music.

The images brought back melodies of the beloved musical tale *Peter and the Wolf* his mother had played when he was a boy. He heard the tunes of the bird and the duck, the cat and the grandfather. The images he saw were the music he heard.

He put the book aside as Bill und Vijay approached and embraced them. When Vijay realized how absorbed in thought Eugen was, he grabbed the book and read its title: *For Inspiration Only.*

„You are looking for inspiration? Then you'll be alright again soon."

But Eugen was anything but inspired. Deep down he felt off his game, but didn't dare show it.

„I am so much better. Give me three more days and I am back to work."

Bill looked at him and laid a hand on his shoulder.

„No, my friend you will take your time. Your body told you a lesson. You are here for a reason.

They sat still. Eugen nodded slowly, he understood. Then Bill took his arm.

„Go to France for a while. See Anna."

And again they sat silent. At last Eugen turned the ring, feeling the allure of Bill's idea. In France were people he liked a lot. There was a way out: Anna.

He seemed to shed a heavy load as his body tightened. Then his cell phone rang and he took his pills.

Vijay pulled printouts from his briefcase and handed them to Eugen.

„Look at these beauties, you'll like them. Your bot sent them."

Eugen looked at the images of a starfish, a star fruit, the star of the Soviets and the star of the US Army.

„The beast is sending me pentagons. "

Vijay: „And lucky you are. At least it doesn't talk Greek anymore."

They laughed, got up and walked through the garden. Then Bill said goodbye. He took the opportunity to visit Betty and Joe.

41

Betty and Joe had come to Venice, California, when the hippies took over the place. Here, the freeway from Hollywood to the Pacific stopped short at a colony of small wooden houses, sometimes painted in a psychedelic manner and with a goat to keep the garden.

Betty und Joe lived on the same street, a short hop from the beach. Joe was grateful for Betty, since he wasn't quick on his feet anymore. But together they were mobile.

Both loved Venice and most of all Venice Beach, the open air spectacle. There were girls in tiny shorts with sassy slogans on their tights, floating on roller skates along the crowded promenade. There were the stars of the basketball courts, showing off. Crowds framed the courts where boom boxes let the air vibrate and roller skaters danced like professionals. Elderly ladies adored young bodybuilders at muscle beach. Beauties idolized men clad in pink suits, neon ties, broad-rimmed hats, bling-bling and patent leather shoes, strutting down the *Ocean Front Walk*.

Betty und Joe were sitting in the sand near the water.

Betty: „I haven't heard of Eugen for weeks, now that I am battling the strangest flaws. Did he fall from a cliff? What's going on?"

„I got a funny feeling. He reminds me of my early days when projects couldn't be too exotic. A run-off-the-mill job for me? Out of the question. I guess, Eugen is still like that. Still wants to be a pioneer and have fun.

„And how did you get your act together?"

„My money ran out. So, I ended up in the industry, working on broadband networks. Wow, this was hot. The Americans bet their last cent on IP, on Internet technology. Not so the Canadians and Europeans. They wanted to play it safe, saddling a new technology, ATM, on the old one. That went down the drain.

It was then that I lost my blinders. I realized that it is an art to make a product: the right thing at the right time and price; and make it maintainable, configurable, safe, operable, and so on."

Joe looked to the ocean letting his memories flow.

„Betty, I don't know what's the matter with Eugen. I only want to know whether he ever launched a product. If not, I am worried."

„A product? I don't think so. He is still wearing blinders. And I tell you, if he doesn't get everything – the perfect bot – he won't care for the rest. I bet if we don't fix the Motivator, he is out."

„And I bet you are right on target, Betty-Baby."

2

The General's Will

The Drôme

Replication

The Deluge

42

In Cairo, the door to an underground garage opened and closed after a rapidly approaching limousine entered. Blindfolded, Alam rose, was led to an elevator and finally found himself in a luxurious apartment. He and his company bowed as a door opened and the General welcomed his guests and asked them into a room furnished with heavy seats around a low table. There was no decoration which could betray the provenance or character of the owner.

They took their seats, were served tea and sweets and exchanged polite small talk, addressing each other by *friend* or *brother*, except for Alam and his contact.

Alam only knew he would meet a general. Now he shook hands with a man in a tailor-made suit who spoke British English faultlessly. Perhaps he was a business man, perhaps he had a military career. Many well-to-do families had moved to Europe after the demise of the Osman Empire, like Alam's family which settled in France. Whether the general descended from Syria, Iraq, Turkey or Lebanon, Alam could infer neither from his appearance, behavior or language. Now the general turned to Alam.

„My secretary tells me, you are bringing us good news. I am glad to hear them. Please speak."

„Your Excellency conveyed interest in a nuclear bomb for tactical deployment. The model I am offering features key advantages. The explosive force varies flexibly in the range up to 700 kilotons, suitable for urban and rural targets. It can be activated remotely via terrestrial and satellite communication. It is of modular design, meaning it is decomposable and highly portable. Its rugged design has been simplified for ease of use: only two months suffice to train your staff. Instruction may start any time and even take place prior to delivery."

Nodding benevolently, the General asked well-informed questions as to the bomb's radioactive footprint – the measurable radiation during and after transport. Then Alan continued:

„Your Excellency, please allow me to propose an innovative concept: It may pique your interest, because a surprise effect can multiply the impact of bombs of smaller size, making them even more versatile.

I am referring to a *double strike* – the strike by a bomb synchronized with a strike which wipes out the communications infrastructure. The physical effects caused by pressure, heat and radiation will be augmented by the chaos and delays when all public and private communication is paralyzed."

The General's face lit up.

„You mean to block the military, police and rescue system?"

„Precisely. Also the press and city management. You name it. "

„Now tell me about the economics."

„The cost of a double strike for a city of 50,000 inhabitants would be less than 20 million dollars, though this is a rough estimate. Of course I can provide you with a detailed cost-benefit analysis."

The General had a sip of tea, reclined, and closed his eyes imagining a double-strike scenario in his mind. He seemed pleased.

„I think a double strike would be very difficult to clear up, which means the power of extortion rises considerably."

„True, Your Excellency, and please don't forget, you could enter history as the inventor of the double strike."

The General smiled. He liked the flexibility of the concept: it wasn't confined to plutonium, it could work with gas and bacteria as well.

„Your Excellency, in case you are interested, I propose a covered test. I am at your service."

„I thank you, Alam, my friend. I am intrigued. Let's begin with a case study. My secretary will reimburse you at once for the splendid work you have done so far. Peace be with you."

The meeting ended. Alam bowed, retired and was blindfolded again.

43

Past midnight, Rachel went down the long corridor to her office, tired and tense. Halfway down she stopped and opened the door to Debbie's realm.

„Still busy with C 121, Debbie?"

„It will be running by Wednesday."

„Good. Super. And now go home. Got me? Go home."

In Rachel's office, folders, manuals, magazines and books, printouts and CDs piled up, the tokens of hard work. A screen showed the restless structure of a bot. Vijay had once joked that bots at Stanford looked cute like Elfs, at MIT ugly like Orks. But Rachel's bot resembled a construction site. She knew all its weak spots and probed them continually. Now she checked the critical ones and sighed with relief – no defects, no alarms. She massaged her temples and relaxed.

Later she deactivated the probes one by one, concluding the tests that had kept her busy for a long time. A few windows remained active, reporting vital functions of the bot. Only a handful of problems had still to be taken care of – minor jobs. Soon she would release this bot-version – the milestone she and her team had pursued relentlessly.

44

Finally, Rachel found time to read her emails and what she read shocked her. She cried *you bastards* ... *schma* ... *oy mame* and slumped. She prayed and calmed down. Finally she used the phone.

„It's me, Rachel ... sorry ... yes, urgent ... not on the phone ... great ... I'll take the early shuttle ... I am so relieved ... bye."

She unplugged a memory stick and disconnected her computer. Then she took the puppet her little daughter had made, pressed it to her cheek, kissed it and left the room. Morning dawned as she crossed the deserted campus on the way to her car, past Gehry's

futuristic buildings. As she cast a last look on the spirit-
ed architecture, her body stretched and her chin rose.

45

Bill met Rachel at the airport and led her to his limousine where the chauffeur was waiting. In the car, Bill
realized how exhausted Rachel was.

Bill: „Take a nap, I'll take you to my home. But
don't be afraid, young lady, Chuck will join us, too."

Later, Chuck, Bill and Rachel had coffee sitting
around the table in Bill's living room.

Bill: „O.k. Rachel, now tell us."

„Bad news."

„Go on. Us old boys can stand it."

„I hope you can. I released a dozen bots."

Chuck: „So, they finally left the lab and are out in
the field. Bravo!"

„They were under way seven weeks, reporting
from Palestine. But at last one bot entered our own
Secret Service. Nothing can stop them."

„That's hot."

„The information I received at midnight was top
secret."

„Well?"

„The bot listed the names of ministers, presidents
princes and other dignitaries surveyed by CIA in the
Middle East."

Chuck whistled.

„Why does it do that?"

„Aha, the million dollar question. If I only knew,
Chuck. It should be doing other things, detect the financial sources of Salafists, for instance."

„This bot is clever, after all."

Rachel realized that Bill und Chuck didn't grasp the consequences. She raised her hands and shook her head.

„Bloody hell. No. I screwed up. I am scared. You hear me? Scared!"

Chuck turned to her.

„Cool it, young lady, we will back you up. Be proud of your bot."

„You cannot help me. And just imagine, somebody else had received the list instead of me."

„Could this happen?"

„Obviously there is a bug. I can't exclude anything. Chuck, bots are so complex and there are so many of them – hundreds."

Bill and Chuck began to grasp the dire situation. Software was always flawed, this they knew only too well. And every bot which replicated, would replicate its flaws.

„What can you do about it?"

„Nothing. They are not like sheep a dog can heard and bring home. They are free – autonomous and, as I said before, nothing can stop them."

They looked upon Rachel, sensing her solitude. Like many programmers she was entirely on her own – trapped by complexity which took its toll. She wasn't even allowed to let others in on bot-technology. Chuck forbade it.

They took a break, had coffee on the veranda and looked to the Appalachian hills in the blue mist, lit by the morning sun. Finally Chuck asked for the worst case and answered, too.

„I guess the worst to happen is that the bots change sides, work against us."

Rachel nodded: „My nemesis."

She closed her eyes and drooped. Bill took her hands and Chuck padded her back.

Chuck: „I am proud of you, gutsy lady. You had the courage to put your cards on the table. Now we can think of how to pull this off. Excuse me."

Chuck was pressed for time and left. Soon after, Rachel and Bill took a break hiking up the hill through untouched forest. Now and then her sight wandered over the trees to the chains of mountains beyond mountains in the west, and this beauty centered her mind. *I have to fix this thing*, she thought, *somehow*.

Rachel: „The bots out there are reproducing like rabbits. If only I could butcher them all."

„Vijay will help. I am sure."

„Oh my god. No. How could I face him after screwing up his work?"

„Easy now. I will handle this. Trust me."

Now Bill had taken command. He would manage the mess and Rachel felt: All was not lost – not yet.

Bill, however, was taking stock. On the positive side: Chuck would check press and police in case information leaked. And Vijay would love to cooperate – he didn't like bots, called them *mercenaries*.

Unfortunately, Vijay had to wipe out all bots to the very last – a single surviving bot would dash all hopes. But would Vijay reach every corner of the Internet? Bill would not bet on it. And Vijay had to find a solution all by himself. Betty and Rachel were familiar with only a fraction of the bot's internal mechanisms. And Eugen was out of reach.

So, Bill feared for the worst, but said nothing about it. He had read in Chuck's face what was at stake, should things go awry.

Perhaps the worst had already happened, rendering Chuck powerless.

46

„At last you are here – let me look at you. Come in, you must be tired."

Anna greeted Eugen with three kisses on the cheeks and led him to his favorite place at the kitchen table.

Eugen: „It was a long flight, but I am not tired, I am just happy to be here again."

Anna had worried. On the phone, Eugen accepted her invitation with an audible sigh of relief. He, whom his job chased around the world incessantly, had time. What happened?

„I am happy, too. I didn't expect you to make time for me."

Eugen spoke about the pitfalls of technology and the momentary pause of the project – a welcome chance to relax after many months of strain.

Anna studied the looks of his face which didn't match his story. Looking on a beaten man she laid her hand on his arm.

„Here, at the piano and in the garden you will leave your bots behind and rest. They are still pestering you – I feel it. And Henri is delighted about your coming. He butchered a duck right away. Look at this beauty."

Eugen shook his head.

„No, I left the bots behind, they are far away by now.“

„I hope they are. But you appear a little bewitched – like the Frog King who has to be kissed by the princess. Ha.“

Days passed with Eugen taking it easy: sleeping, hiking, playing piano. Jean came to visit and his kids played with uncle Eugen. Still, he did not recuperate, remained sad and listless.

Nothing distracted him. He did not fiddle with software anymore, did not study the daily flow of error messages produced by Rachel's tests, did not devise solutions and organize repair. An empty day lay before him every morning.

One evening, after a glass of wine, he tried to reconstruct the dark days of Stanford, but – his memory giving out – he got nowhere.

Anna was concerned because he ate and talked little and was taking medicine she didn't know.

„Look, Eugen, many people are suffering a crisis and get over it. Some relieve their soul by writing about their burden. Some draw and paint to express what troubles them deep down. Some simply talk about what is depressing them and get rid of it.

Tell me about your bot. What was the crux of the matter?“

Eugen tended to push this question aside, feeling too sore to scrutinize what had brought him to his knees. Now, he looked at Anna and her compassion cheered him up.

„Interrupt me if I bore you with technical details.“

„I will. I am listening.“

„One component of the bot I called *Motivator*. It's a lofty name for a component which does little more than allocate needed resources to fellow components. In a way, it distributes the energy to do a job.

To kick off, a job needs storage space, computing time and lots of rights: rights to use a service, rights to start a task or to cancel it again. Without such resources a bot is unable, i.e. unmotivated, to do anything. O.k.?"

„An example would help."

„For instance, the Motivator allocates computing time to the *Goaler*, which determines the bot's goals: what should the bot do next – find information about a terrorist or something else?

Once the Goaler determines what to do, the planer determines how to do it, the steps and actions to reach the goal. Bots usually screen the computers of a suspect and those of his partners as well as the archives of the police. Thus bots are working off long lists of tasks."

„So, your bot could have inspected my computer, read my private mail and then told you about me?"

„Of course he could have. It's easy but improbable. Besides, you would not have noticed. Bots are nosey but well-behaved."

Anna was not amused:

„Hm. He never gets out of hand?"

„Rarely. A kind of superego controls him, the *Introspector*, again a flowery name for a piece of software. Sigmund Freud would suspect it at once, ha. It checks that a bot doesn't fool around or squander resources."

Anna was impressed by her glimpse of a strange new world, but wondered:

„So, bots function like clockwork. Now, where is your problem?"

„One problem is, the Motivator grants resources not only to others, but also to himself. Otherwise he could not work. The question is: how much? Imagine, the Motivator was a banker who decides on his own bonuses.

„I am beginning to understand."

„Wait, there is more: The Introspector must control everything. But should he also control himself? Think of Louis XIV, the Sun King and one-man Supreme Court. He never judged himself but probably should have.

Believe me, a greedy Motivator and a permissive Introspector may cause a lot of harm."

Anna filled the glasses.

„Drink. It's last year's wine. It has already developed character and may become a vintage wine."

Eugen was glad for this break, since his dark memories were flashing up again. But Anna pushed on:

„Now tell me what happened. You failed, didn't you? I read it in your face."

She touched him again and he looked at her, feeling safe.

„My project is stuck for good. This is bad enough but the worst is, I don't fully understand why I failed and it is giving me nightmares."

Anna pitied him and thought about the Motivator and the Introspector, these strange creatures which must work on themselves.

Then the old paradox came to her mind: *All Cretans are liars. I am a Cretan.* 2600 years ago, the disciples of the philosopher Parmenides racked their brains over it. Were all Cretans liars indeed, or was this a lie? After all it may have been an untruthful Cretan who said it. But was the man Cretan? Perhaps not, he may have lied about himself. Anna:

„Could your bot suffer from a vicious cycle of the *I am a Cretan liar* kind and lying to itself. Or I am a Motivator and motivating myself, I am an Introspector and inspecting myself? Self-references tend to be diabolical."

„Perhaps vicious cycles are diabolic. In any case, they exist in human brains. We call them neuroses. Were they diabolic, the human race would have become extinct long ago. Our brains are wonderfully tolerant, they easily put up with contradictions. Unfortunately, my bots' brains are not as powerful. Not yet."

„Are your bots stranded?"

„Presently yes, in future perhaps."

„What are you going to do about it?"

„I don't know."

Eugen breathed heavily and Anna took him in her arms.

47

Henri was the first man Eugen had come to know and like in the Drôme. That he was married to the charming and warmhearted Marie-Thérèse revealed much about the farmer and hobby-stargazer.

Though Henri und Eugen could not converse in a common language they got closer. They jointly repaired old machines at low cost and worked in the vegetable field where artichokes, peas, melons, and onions grew between long rows of gladiolas.

Eugen installed a discarded computer at Henri's house and introduced him to the Internet. Henri who had recently retired, now began the day by visiting NASA's *Astronomy Picture Of the Day* and studying the wonderful images of sun, Saturn, satellites, spacecraft, nebulae and galaxies.

Marie Thérèse got used to summon him for breakfast when he was immersed into the descriptions provided by astronomers and cosmologists. He translated them automatically into French, and when the translation did not work out properly, he used dictionaries and his imagination. Intrigued by Wolf-Rayet stars and gravitational lenses he would easily forget about breakfast.

Henri's English language skills progressed, now that Anna had lent him a book that had started her love of English when she was a girl. Henri, too, would be captured by Jack London's *Call of the Wild*. And he was.

Eugen questioned Anna about Henri, whose children lived in distant cities and whose strength was fading. What when the last cow was sold?

„Soon he will give up the toil in the vineyard, even his beloved boar hunting. But he will be alright – take care of the house and the garden and keep one field."

„He will show me the mushrooms, cèpes in fall and morels in spring."

„Even morels? He must really like you."

Eugen looked out the window and beyond the garden to the foothills bordering the big river valley. He thought of the old farms in the neighborhood and the people taking pride in their own wine and cheese. Here, he could live.

48

In next to no time, Rachel and her students prepared rooms for Vijay; one room to work in and one to rest. Nothing would distract him here in MIT's basement.

When Vijay, who had just arrived, knocked on Rachel's open door she cried out in relief.

„There you are. I could not wait."

As she looked away from him shamefully, Vijay bowed.

„At your service, milady. But I am surprised: nothing is happening here. I guessed you were sitting amongst all your little darlings, playing with bots on your lap."

„Don't rub it in. I feel miserable."

„Little wonder: you invited a mass murderer. I'll butcher them all … the great massacre of the bots … streams of bot-blood flowing in the streets."

„Stop it, will you? And now come with me. No time to lose. I'll show you the dungeons."

Vijay entered a windowless room, sparsely furnished with desk, whiteboard, computers and fridge.

„Ah, the InterContinental. Looks perfect for a weekend escape."

„Nothing will keep you from working."

Then she opened the door to the adjacent room.

„Voilá the Indian parlor."

It took Vijay's breath away. Indian figurines, lamps and carpets, soft seats and cushions on a grand bed created a cozy exotic ambience. Nothing was missing. A screen showed a Bollywood movie and a guitar leaned on an armchair. Vijay gently touched a Buddha statue.

„Who did this?"

„My students, your service team. They are dying to meet the superstar of Stanford."

Vijay felt at home when the students appeared, Dipal und Nomita, and soon laughed with them.

His delicate task challenged Vijay brutally. At any time of day he could be found programming. Usually he was talking to himself, uttering phrases like: *now sverc-trac ... shit didn't sync ... no match here... shift up one tier ... zaro-activation ... too early again ... damn ... broke the loop ... not this way.* Nomita and Dipal served food and drink, removed used dishes, came and left noiselessly, unnoticed.

49

Nomita and Dipal often served Indian food they had prepared for their countryman and when one evening Vijay smelled fresh curry he quit his work and the three of them dined in the Indian room.

The students were curious why Vijay had come to MIT and was working like mad. Rachel had not told them anything. Now Nomita turned to him.

„How secretive you are."

„Indeed? Well, I guess I am. And you want to know what I am doing. I am interested in pattern recognition, working on a scanner in fact. Nothing special – they have been built for decades and recognize audio and visual patterns reliably. But you know all of this, don't you."

„DNA patterns too? You are a geneticist after all."

„Yes, progress was immense, stunning algorithms sped things up by orders of magnitude."

„What's left to be done then?"

Vijay sensed he had teated these kind young people unfairly and had better tell them a trifle.

„There is a class of patterns which we cannot match and recognize well, not like sounds or molecules. You could call them logic patterns. But I can't tell you more because I am hunting for a patent. Thus, not a word to anybody. Promise?"

The students promised with a heavy heart since Vijay had not satisfied but stimulated their curiosity.

„But a professor in the dungeons. Why?"

„Dungeons? Not at all. The service couldn't be better."

Vijay grabbed the guitar, played Indian tunes, sang, and the students joined in.

Then he delved into his work again – software to determine the presence of a bot in a computer. It reminded him of scifi movies where scanners determined the presence of life-forms on a space ship.

Vijay shared the fate of many developers of complex algorithms: being entirely on his own. Even the best students at MIT would need many weeks to familiarize themselves with his task, let alone help him.

Such *intellectual solitude*, as he called it, mattered little to him. But he felt hard-pressed since he had not found the patterns of a bot he could use like a fingerprint.

For years he had pursued his hobby: finding characteristic structures of cognition in human and animal brains. Yet he didn't find any and gave up. His colleagues, too, neurologists at the medical faculty, who studied the architecture of the human brain and tried to map out its functional design, had given up.

But lately he had scrutinized the reasoning mechanisms of bots, which is structure par excellence. Eugen had wondered about his abnormal interest in inference procedures. Then they had talked for hours about the essence of reasoning, but in the end could not define it.

So, patterns of cognition were out. Vijay's hope now lay in patterns of replication. Rachel's bots spread, thanks to the reproduction mechanism he had installed in them. It worked recursively, copying a bot by composing all its parts from smaller parts over many tiers of composition – except for one anomaly: the copier copied itself.

Vijay believed he would be able to detect and use this anomaly as the fingerprint. But it would not be easy.

50

Nomita und Dipal wondered a little more every day as they caught glimpses of Vijay's screens. One screen looked like their own work station screen. But another looked weird and eerie – showing how Vijay's killer operated within a bot.

The killer – reddish implants deep down in the three-dimensional maze of bots – looked like germs gnawing on tissue. When the killer became active, the bot reacted: its structure wobbled and its colors pulsed. It sometimes shrunk, lost cohesion and crumbled.

Sometimes the bot's activity escalated, colors pulsing feverishly, until it collapsed into a heap of lifeless shards. The bot also seemed to voice its feelings during these scenes: it sighed, groaned, growled, grunted and shrieked. The students didn't know what to make of it.

Vijay was reading the message *exit_7317_seq29*, when Rachel entered and whispered *everything alright, my friend?* She left as Vijay babbled, lost in thought. Rachel appeared changed – less driven, caring.

51

Eugen had changed as well by dropping his roles of project manager and chief architect of bots. His passion for gambling faded; the French way of life appealed to him.

He watched Anna cutting and cleaning chicken, brought sage, thyme and tarragon from the garden, and peeled garlic for lunch.

„Anna, there is something I want to show you. My bot sent it."

„He sent you *something?* Don't you know what it is?"

„I am at my wits' end, once again."

Anna studied the laptop on the kitchen table, displaying the line *Protrepticos* above Greek text and ending with *beautiful.*

„Oh, it looks like a famous piece of philosophy. Let me check."

She read the text and translated:

„Everything created by human skill is created for a purpose which is its goal and its best. But what is created by chance does not fulfill an objective. A good thing may result from chance but it is not good because of chance. Because what results from chance remains indeterminate in all cases. ... The honorable man who

121

leads his life according to good thinking, will not fall victim to chance…"

„Truly beautiful it is."

Anna noticed Eugen ridiculing her in his own helpless way.

„What sense of beauty did you implant your bot? You programmed it."

Totally at a loss, Eugen swore he hadn't implanted anything of the kind, neither the concept of beauty nor a method to detect or enjoy beauty, or to talk about it. Any sense of beauty was utterly irrelevant when fighting terror.

„But it said *beautiful* and probably meant *Protrepticos is beautiful.*"

„Merely a quirk, I guess, or a case of sloppy programming."

The bot was young and error-prone. Rachel had tested all bots, but not this one. This bot went its own ways for months, occasionally giving notice, usually from a library. Perhaps, it was like a wayward child and a little queer.

Eugen also thought of his new architecture, the *Society of Mind*, which Vijay disrespectfully called *Society of Spirits*. Was it flawed?

Suddenly Eugen's doubts and dark memories were back, haunting him once more. Only Anna's company and a long walk would settle his mind again. He reached for his boots, inviting Anna to come with him to *Saint Jean de Fromental*, the little chapel in the nearby hills where pilgrims had come to rest for centuries.

Anna welcomed the hike to clear her mind. What she had just learned had raised her interest. This scouting young bot, perhaps still *in puberty*, was doing astounding things. She was reminded of her first philosophy teacher, a Jesuit scholar, who discussed Protrepticos with passion. And she recalled that after her initial problems, Protrepticos had revealed to her the road to philosophy. Only then she had grasped its beauty.

What was it, then, the bot termed *beautiful*? Was it the charm of language, the power of argument, the appeal of *good thinking* or else?

As they wandered along, Eugen mentioned the bot had sent various messages, all of them cryptic and impossible to fathom. The other day it had sent pentagrams in form of flowers, blossoms and fruits. And, at the end of each message, it added the word *beautiful*.

Anna: „A pentagram is a simple graph, but regular and balanced, even symmetrical, and a symbol used in many cultures. Anybody may like it. Bots, too, I assume."

„Granted. But a pentagram and Protrepticos – why these beauties appeal to a bot, I can't make out."

„I can't make out anything either. And I can't help thinking of C3PO, the golden droid in *Star Wars*. It deemed itself beautiful, irresistibly elegant."

„C3PO is a freaky type – cheeky, scared and vain. But people love its quirks, which lets me hope for my bot."

They reached the chapel, went up the steps through an iron gate, circled the tiny building and sat down on the bench sheltered by the low roof.

Anna began to reflect on concepts the bot had used much to her surprise. Passing through the hard school of philosophy she had learned to care for the precise meaning of words. She had even published a paper on the concept *freedom* which changed its meaning profoundly and repeatedly over the course of centuries.

The bot had sent a piece of text dealing with the concepts *good* and *chance* above all. But why? And what might their meaning be for a machine?

Eugen was certain the bot knew nothing about *good*. Such fuzzy metaphysics were not helpful, even detrimental. But Anna pushed on.

„What about *chance*?"

„That's a very different matter. The bot knows that chance can affect it any time – simple programming errors may cripple or kill it."

„Does it fear chance which can work out for or against it?"

A bot which fears – what a strange idea, Eugen thought, *my bot fearful like C3PO?* He laughed and then mused.

„Well, meanwhile it seems I cannot say anything with certainty about this strange beast. It seems to enjoy beautiful things, however. And who enjoys may fear as well."

On their way back, Anna let her thoughts run freely and was toying with concepts. Eugen listened in awe: no doubt, Anna had learned to think in a different manner.

52

Henri visited Anna in her library, in his hand her book, which he had read with pleasure. He brought it back asking for another, equally entertaining and easy to read. He considered buying an e-book, to find the

French meaning of an English word with one click. But he decided on a printed book because he wrote new vocabulary into a booklet which he read again and again. English, language of the historic archenemy, appealed to him, and he wanted to converse with Eugen – at least well enough to ask him about his work. As yet, Anna hadn't satisfied his curiosity.

„What does the man do?“

Anna: „He is an Internet specialist. Makes Software.“

„What kind of software?“

„I guess it protects the Internet from aggressors.“

„Criminals? Terrorists? In the *Semaine de la Drôme* I read they are dangerous.“

„You are right. Jean said this, too.“

„Eugen travels a lot. Where is his home? Will he stay now? I hope he will. He is a nice guy.“

„I, too, hope he will stay a while.“

„Does his software protect well?“

„It's a little sick, I believe.“

„Got a tummy ache? Ha-ha.“

„That's not what I meant. It's bonkers. Needs help.“

„From a psychiatrist?“

„I guess so.“

„My brother, Auguste, was crazy, too, and Dr. Philibert helped him.“

„How is he now?“

„Well. He is working again and he loves his wife.“

„What did Dr. Philibert do?“

„Not much. He talked and talked with Auguste, told him he will heal himself. And so it came.“

„Hopefully, Eugen's software will repair itself also."

„And now give me another book, please."

Anna handed him *Tortilla Flat* by John Steinbeck. Later Ernest Hemingway's *The Old Man and the Sea* would follow.

53

The black currant, queen of berries, was ready for harvest in the Drôme. People spent more time in the garden than usual, picking ripe berries only. They are boiled down according to old recipes passed from mothers to daughters. Anna had learned the secrets of cassis jelly from her grandmother at her kitchen stove. She never revealed the spices she used, nor how she added the taste of grapes in the fall. Cassis, they said, shortens the winter.

Again, Eugen was helping in the kitchen, chatting and watching Anna cook – a welcome diversion since he considered his grand game lost. He would never bring his bots to perfection, he feared, nor finish his theory. This was bad enough. But his bot spoke to him in riddles, leaving him clueless which was worse. And would he ever stop sending beauties?

„Anna, what is beauty?"

Anna stopped and turned to him, smiling. Finally he had come up with a question which could help him on.

„This I can't tell you. But don't be sad. Look what the great thinkers did when they were at a loss. They discussed concepts with students and followers, sometimes in the shade of trees, in galleries and at universities. Then concepts like *freedom*, *justice* and *good* took shape.

You can do this, too. Come with me, join my seminar and ask your question."

„Like: what means *kalós kai agathós*?"

Eugen had not forgotten the expression. Its strong rhythm reminded him of the beat of a Russian dance. And he could not figure out what the old Greeks meant by it.

54

Buried in work as usual, Vijay suddenly relaxed his strained face. He was finished, his killer fully on target. He stretched, jumped up and called Rachel.

„Ready for the night of the long knives? My killer works splendidly or should I say *deadly*. Still, I am afraid."

When Rachel appeared, Vijay explained:

„When you release them, the world will rock. These beasts multiply in a chain reaction. We will witness a monster show."

Mother Nature had told him how to replicate. And though he could not match the replication speed of algae, he came close to it. It would bring the Internet down.

Rachel listened with interest and without scruples. She was ready to risk everything except lives. So it would happen tonight. Finally.

She had prepared a dozen launch pads in different parts of the country. They would release the killers at precisely the same time. No one would suspect her institute as the source of the avalanche: it would be stifled, just as the entire MIT.

55

In the early hours of the day the doors had opened for Vijay's beasts. As they swarmed, Rachel retired to her office and slept untill the morning. Then she went over to Debbie to find out what had happened during the night.

Debbie had been studying the logs of the network since midnight. Now she showed Rachel a time-lapse video.

„Look, traffic as usual at midnight. And then at 2:26 the net starts going haywire. Wild peaks, reaching a maximum after 217 seconds. Then the alarm. Look over here: all routers are blinking. Overload. Then it happens, the main connector goes down: at 2:31 MIT disconnected."

„Any news from abroad?"

„Nothing. I usually listen to public radio news on the way in, but heard music only, not one spoken word. And down at the news stand are yesterday's papers only. So, no news today."

„What now?"

„Don't ask me It's not natural. The net never went down like that before. But it will come back for sure. Trust me."

„Take a break and take the day off."

Happily, Debbie agreed, leaving Rachel behind, now shocked by the eerie situation and fearing the day.

56

Baffled students crowded Rachel's office, the TV turned to CNN, the only channel on air, though apparently in emergency mode. On *Good Morning America* merely headlines displayed: *Torrents of information gushing world-wide ...dramatic decline of Internet services continues ... all security agencies, military forces and NATO alerted ... the phenomenon is being investigated ... no official statements yet.*

A telephone interview with the Secretary of the Interior followed. Clumsily, he stated that he was not in a position to provide pertinent information but all things necessary were being done. His ministry would keep the considerate public updated on the current state of affairs ... and the public should remain calm.

After all, the Internet had been designed to resist nuclear attacks. It was, in fact, the world's most resilient technical system.

People came to Rachel's office and left, learned bits and pieces of what was going on. The cables on the Atlantic floor were intact but the giant network nodes in London and Frankfurt inoperable, Europe had been cut off since 5:07 GMT. Network performance in the Middle East was severely throttled and dysfunction in the Far East mounting.

All sorts of plants and services were affected: energy supply, health care, banking, and communications. Miraculously, a few satellite connections remained untouched.

CNN switched to the White House, for the first press release. The speaker reported that network overload, congestion and failure had commenced some six hours ago in several areas simultaneously. Since then, experts had worked feverishly to uncover the cause, so far however without tangible results. Evidence increased that the word was faced with an entirely new type of phenomenon; no computer, processor and operating system, being immune.

Most puzzling was the speed of its which eliminated conventional malware like viruses as a cause. No residues of computer code had been found, yet, a fact which ran counter to practical wisdom. It mystified scientists who, at present, could not exclude anything, not even terrorism.

57

Finally, Vijay appeared well-rested and in a good mood. People watched him curiously and Rachel was glad to see him.

„Vijay, this is a deadlocked institute. Downtime for all but the TV."

„No no no, it's a chance. I'll call the caterer. Let's have lunch together and have fun. I want to pay back my guardian angels. Nomita and Dipal, you helped me survive the dungeons. Let's party at lunch."

Everyone cheered. Then they urged him to talk about his work. Rumors had spread about strange ongoings in the basement but leaving everyone in the dark. Now there was time enough to socialize and talk.

Vijay: „With pleasure, my friends. We could talk about replication, if you like. It is a hot topic nowadays. I'll meet you around 11."

The office emptied and Vijay turned to Rachel who hunched over the keyboard, scanning old and forgotten emails only to distract her mind of the grim forebodings she had seen. He pitied her, trying to cheer her up:

„I bet the evening news will be quite entertaining. All sorts of experts will air their fancy theories."

Rachel did not react but gladly accepted his invitation to join his lecture, which had already been announced:

Special Lecture on
Replication of Monocellular Algae
Prof. Vijay Ch. Yunus
Director Computational Genetics Center
Stanford University, CA.
Today, 11:15, Room 702.

The room was crowded as Vijay began to show his slides.

„Red Algae reproduce terribly fast, inexplicably fast to tell the truth. Look here: reddish sea water. Algae did it virtually overnight. See this minuscule creature? This tiny beast is the culprit. Guess their number – billions, trillions, quadrillions …?

How can this miracle happen? I guess the answer lies in the genes. That's what we geneticists always believe. So, we do what we always do: read the genes, analyze and compare them, observe them in action, watch them duplicate.

Or we use our imagination and that's what we did. We built a computer model of a simple alga. Then we simulated how it replicates given certain conditions of temperature, light, nutrients, carbon, oxygen, minerals. Replication worked indeed, much to our surprise, but only slowly.

131

We learned more as we focused on structure exclusively. Our assumption was: some cell structures replicate more easily, i.e. consume less energy, than others. The underlying question was: how to optimize cell structure to speed up replication?"

The audience was excited. It sensed that software may have clogged the Internet. If so, replication may have played a role. How else could it have happened?

Student: „Would the optimization of structure also apply to software structure?"

Vijay perceived the hidden danger of the question. The last thing he wanted to do was talk about software, his current project. He had better confine the discussion to research and biology.

„Software? That would be difficult to say. We are still struggling to come to grips with the basics in biology. Look at these two structures. Both replicate. The one on the left needs 10% less energy and replicates 30% faster than the right one. But why? Both look pretty similar. So we must dig down, understand the chemistry for instance. But more than that: we must understand the essence of design – its elegance, effectiveness, simplicity. That's where we will find the answer, I guess.

Student: „I am Sonja. I don't get it. What elegance?"

„Sorry Sonja. Think of the Brooklyn Bridge and its wonderful elegance. Look it up on the Internet. For a long time people thought a bridge like that could never be built. And then a man designed the perfect structure: light-weight, strong and beautiful. A structural breakthrough. Did this help, Sonja?"

„O.k. thanks Vijay."

„Of course we hope for a quantum leap, even hope to beat the algae, but there is a long way ahead of us. Progress moves like a snail, they say."

The audience listened spellbound, but then grew restless. It felt as if the quantum leap was imminent. Vijay had conveyed much less than he knew. A discussion broke out: *How can software replicate? What's the functional nucleus? How to distribute replication? ...*

Vijay felt cornered, ready for an escape.

„Ok, ok. Easy, folks, easy, don't overshoot. Besides, it's lunchtime now. The buffet is downstairs. Follow me now."

58

Rachel, Debbie and Vijay gathered in front of the TV, nervous and tense. The evening news would handle one topic only: the mystery of the Internet. It would be overwhelming: the avalanche they had triggered would come down on them. Now, the anchorman appeared:

„Ladies and gentlemen, today the world witnessed a man-made phenomenon as inconceivable and powerful as the first atomic bomb. A virtual tsunami rocked and shattered the Internet. A flash flood of data sped through its fibers and cables. The Internet has crashed. It is down. New York and San Francisco, Tokyo and Shanghai are offline."

Vijay: „Wow, what a poet. I love the lyrics of this stanza. Too bad, the second stanza will be shabby prose. He'll tell us we are hunting a phantom and we will overcome."

Vijay was already getting bored. He had foreseen it. Debbie on the other hand who only had a vague idea of Vijay's mission and work remained glued to the news, trying to make sense of a day which had started so violently for her network. Rachel, finally, envied Vijay. How could he stay so aloof, so utterly detached? She was involved body and soul. All statements and images sank in. She, not Vijay, was the final cause of what was happening. And she would probably see more than she could take.

She gazed at the video showing the empty trading floor of the New York Stock Exchange, then at the agitated masses in front of it.

„A sensation happened, the New York Stock Exchange remained closed on an ordinary working day, after trading had stopped in Tokyo. Then the capital markets called it a day. Listen now as the President of Unitrade rates the odds:"

„The stock market will lose a trifle, half a trillion dollars or more. But it may recover. Everything depends on the duration of the Internet crisis. Let's hope it vanishes quickly."

Rachel breathed deeply on this first bit of good news: the world would eventually recover. Somehow.

Then the White House came into focus – men in uniform, road blocks, police vehicles, antennas and transmission gear. A helicopter swept in. Then the press secretary went up to the microphone:

„Ladies and gentlemen, security experts predicted an assault on the Internet. Whether it happened today, we don't know. The security advisor to the President does not exclude an immediate threat. This is why the President is not at the White House, but in a safe place. Mr. President will address the nation tonight …"

The press was craving for news, but the speaker had nothing to offer – no hypothesis, no suspicion, not even a hint. The journalists were livid and shouting: „*Washington's asleep! … Go to hell! … Bunch of Losers! … Washout! … Go and ask the Israelis!*

When it was time for the world news, a photo showed the futuristic BMW-building next to the factory gate where hundreds of workers were leaving the plant. Then the audio link went live:

„The BMW-plants here in Munich are not humming any longer. They came to a full stop. Car assembly depends on a myriad of suppliers. They supply *just in time*. The Internet is what keeps them in sync. If it fails, assembly continues for six hours. This time has passed and the assembly line has stopped. In fact all assembly lines may have stopped in Germany and perhaps even in China. Randy Ametsbichler from Munich."

The channel switched to a reporter on a hotel's top floor with a grandiose view of Cairo at dawn.

„The pace of life in the entire East seems reduced, almost paralyzed, except perhaps for Iran, about which I know nothing. The countries between Morocco and Iraq, the Gulf States, Israel and Egypt are out of touch. Email, file transfer and so forth are dead. Only one satellite link is still operational, otherwise I could not speak to you, and two vintage radio stations are still on the air. And if not a few telex machines weren't still connected to public agencies as they have since the 1960s, I would have little to tell you."

Rachel looked at the vast city sprawling on the banks of the Nile in the soft morning light. Cairo seemed at peace and she felt relief. Then the speaker continued:

„Officials are reluctant to comment on the situation, though the rumor mill is working overtime. No doubt, it was an innovative super-high-tech attack. Only a few countries, or the international mafia are capable of it."

The speaker was interrupted, reached for a sheet of paper, and went on:

„I just received information that Israel has begun to mobilize. Sid Seybold from Cairo."

Rachel closed her eyes and drooped.

„Oh my god. I can't bear any more of this."

Vijay: „It's tough for you, I know. And you haven't eaten all day. Take a break now. Let's all go down to the dungeons. There are still leftover delicacies from lunch"

Rachel's spirit rose as they were sitting in the Indian room, devouring what they found in the fridge while Vijay played the guitar. This peaceful shelter helped Rachel unwind.

Finally Debbie summoned up her courage, booted a workstation and realized, MIT's intranet was running again. She even received the popular TV series *Ask the Dude*. Perfect! They put up their feet, leaned back and watched the woman reporter hunting for people's gut reactions in the streets of New York:

„What do you say about the Internet going down?"

„Technology got out of hand. First, a Space Shuttle crashed, then the blackout of the electric grid. Now the Internet. It's a bloody mess. Nobody gives a damn any more. Greed, greed, greed. Bankers are the worst. Screw'em!"

„Frankly, I am stumped. But it looks like an alien attack. Appears from nowhere. Leaves no trace. It's so different. Extraterrestrial."

„It's the first plague sent by God Almighty to a world of sinners. Mind my words! Repent!"

He pulled a book from his pocket and held it to the camera.

„Here, the Book of Revelation. Read the Lord's word. Read and repent you sinners!"

Even Rachel was amused. Then the camera switched over to Ground Zero in New York where hundreds of people gathered again to stand up against evil. And again they grasped hands singing *we shall overcome.*

Vijay switched the TV off.

„We did it, Rachel. It's over: the bots are dead and the Internet lives."

They stood in silence for a moment, looking at each other. Then Rachel gave Vijay high-five and went her way. There was someone she wanted to call.

„It's me, Rachel. Bill you got it for sure, the whole world was under water ... Yes, of course, it's on my account ... But don't worry, we pulled it off. It's over now ... Bill I did my best to dodge the NSA ... And tell Chuck to keep his eyes open ... Thank you so much, my friend. Bye now."

59

After Vijay stopped working in the dungeons, Dipal und Nomita began to restore the Indian room and the killer-workshop. And they remembered details they had gathered of Vijay, the mysterious man.

137

According to his creed, he belonged to a poor minority in India. Amazing, that he had made it to Stanford. He had mastered computers and yet kept them at bay. He was not one of the ubiquitous evangelists of computerism. Instead he loved the biology of life and models of cooperation in society. But his personal goal remained hidden like so many other things: *Why is Vijay leaving now? Was his work ready to be patented? Or did Rachel cause his demise? She appeared to be reborn after the breakdown of the Internet.*

Vijay and Rachel had come down, too, to clean the computers. No trace should betray what had happened. Nomita and Dipal would probably be the detectives giving in to the curiosity they could hardly hide.

Vijay was well aware how attached they were to him although he had blatantly tricked them.

„Come and see me at Stanford. Then I can pay you back a bit. Stay the next term if you wish."

„You bet we wish."

Excited, they brought him the guitar.

„Play for our goodbye, please."

Vijay played and sang *If You Can Believe Your Eyes and Ears*. Rachel who had grown up with this tune of *The Mamas and The Papas* sang second voice. But Nomita und Dipal wondered why Vijay played this unknown song. Was he telling them something – not to give away what they may have heard and seen? With a cheerful goodbye, the students left.

Rachel was humming songs like *Midnight Voyage* until nothing reminded of the deluge of bots. And she was curious:

„How on earth did you target the bots? Each one could be configured in a different way on a different computer. Did you use birdshot?"

„A killer proceeds in five steps: first invade a computer, then recognize a bot's presence, then deactivate it, then remove the vital parts. And at last the killer removes itself."

„Wow. And this works reliably?"

„A tiny marker betrays a bot's presence reliably and is easy to spot. The rest is messy – must deal with machine code, ugly stuff."

„And then you plucked it out of the bowels of the machine"

„Oh no. That would be impossible. I only made sure the thing was dead and would never come to life again. Shot it between the eyes, ha."

Rachel rested on a seat, pondering what unsettled her.

„The bots have not been removed – neither burned nor buried?"

„True."

„Then the Internet is like a battlefield, filled with millions of corpses of bots."

„True, also. But only for a short time: every restart of a computer will bury a bot. And no relics will remain, no bones, no pacemakers, no gold crowns."

Rachel worried that the bots would leave traces – by travelling through the network and, shockingly, even after their death.

Still, Rachel trusted Vijay much more than she ever trusted Eugen. He had delivered a masterpiece and almost become a friend. Now she invited him to lunch at D'Amelio's and they drove down to the harbor.

60

Vijay surprised Rachel time and again. She had expected him to be mad at her, but he proved a good sport – like a chess player out to win the tournament. Now they were dining *seafood fresh from the boat* and Rachel addressed the situation.

„Are you sad, the project stranded the way it did?"

„To tell the truth, I don't care for bots. But I care for something else. Eugen, our master, calls it knowledge architecture, his pride and joy."

„Amazing. I never heard of it."

„Little wonder, he rarely talked about it by choice and if he did, he was hard to understand. Even I don't understand him, though I questioned him for hours. But I feel he found a golden nugget which should not get lost.

He often said the Internet appalled him. It was a gold mine for humans but merely a waste dump for machines, filled with snippets of text and splinters of knowledge, nothing but flotsam and jetsam. What a waste it was. Since the Middle Ages knowledge has been highly valued, even considered holy. Every library was a piece of art and even more so the encyclopedias which collected and ordered knowledge with love and respect. But these times were gone and Eugen was sad about it, very sad.

He talked about the idea of ordering all knowledge of mankind and representing it *canonically*, which, I guess, meant systematically. He wanted to aggregate facts by following rules a computer could understand.

Once he said, an isolated piece of knowledge is worth nothing. It must find its proper place within all the other pieces. I guess he wanted to integrate all knowledge into one big unit with billions of parts which all interrelate. "

Rachel: „Like a very big computer brain?"

„Probably. But there seemed to be more.

This knowledge must not be composed at random like in a convoluted brain, nor be interlinked at random, like in today's Internet. There had to be architecture – rules of order – a *canon* as he called it."

„My god, it's overwhelming. Why didn't he ever mention it when he talked about bots?"

„Rachel, this is just between you and me. I guess this knowledge architecture was at the core of his theory – bots were only a means to an end. He needed them to prove the knowledge architecture worked. You cared to protect your kin. He didn't care for anything like that.

Perhaps it was this theory, not the misery of bots, which drove him mad."

Rachel regretted that she had invited Vijay on the very last day before he left. There were so many things which only he knew – things she never cared for and which no test could tell. She felt ashamed of her naïveté. She had launched the bots without a clue what it meant to understand bots. She even despised Eugen, this most amazing man, who was not to blame.

The dessert had been delicious and the meal a delight and now they were finishing it with coffee and almond liqueur. Rachel had gained much insight she hadn't expected, but still felt at a loss: what about the *knowledge architecture*, the key to Eugen's approach. She asked Vijay for an example.

„Let's take your institute as an example. It is not easy to comprehend. There are buildings, rooms, furniture, devices – many things we can touch and which all have color, size, weight and many other properties. 100,000 facts about them you can put into a bot. O.k.?

„Yes, of course."

„But there are many other things also. There are the special methods and databases the institute applies to solve problems. Think of the computer programs you apply to test bots. These things are of a different nature: you cannot touch them. Hardware can fall on your foot, software can't. They belong to different categories Eugen kept strictly apart.

And so on. The institute has rights and duties, assets and debts, contracts, patents and licenses. Such knowledge belongs to yet another category. Your duties as a director are neither hardware nor software. And think of all the projects and processes – the myriad of ongoings and the continuous change. So, there are more categories."

„And millions of facts, no doubt."

„Indeed. And they must all be in order. If you tell your bot: *My institute has blue children*, it should realize you are talking nonsense or making fun. If a bot accepted garbage like that it would produce nothing but garbage."

„Bingo. And Eugen solved the garbage problem?"

„I guess he did. He loved categories and believed us to be lost without them. By the way, your institute abounds with structures: buildings, projects, software, contracts and financial plans have structure. His bot was trained to recognize and analyze all kinds of structure."

„Enough, enough, I am beginning to grasp what it means to capture an institute."

61

Vijay's time was up and Rachel driving him to Logan Airport.

Rachel: „What a pity I never came to know Eugen the way you did."

„Then you would admire him as I do. This man lives his idea and what an idea it is. It took me months to find out. He didn't confide in anybody, nor share his thoughts. But after a number of cocktails at the Faculty Club he opened up.

Then he talked to me about his wonderful teacher named Siebenlist, who studied in Berlin and later emigrated from Germany. He tried to teach Eugen Latin and Greek. I imagine Papa Stalin didn't favor such bourgeois behavior. Thus, Siebenlist risked his life and eventually lost it. But before he was executed, he introduced Eugen to the Aristotelian categories, one of the great achievements of mankind.

Later Eugen tried to integrate Aristotelian wisdom into his theory. He said he felt like a mountaineer who knows about the impossible routes to a mountain top and believes in a new route: difficult and risky, but elegant and inviting and to be tackled with Aristotle's help at last. Rachel, he had to climb this route - it called out to him irresistibly.

„The knowledge architecture?"

„Yes. It should become the keystone in the grand arch which starts from naked hardware and reaches intelligent behavior. And only if knowledge was perfected, he believed, bots would think flawlessly and learn with incredible speed."

„So, he didn't do it for the fun of it?"

„Need drove him, I guess."

Vijay looked at Rachel nodding and indicating she had touched on the core of the matter.

„Precisely. *Without the knowledge architecture, introspection will never work*, he once remarked, *this needs perfection*."

„And why is this?"

„Rachel, I wish I had understood more of it."

3

Seminar of Philosophy

Conclave of Venice

Number of Life

Blog of a Bot

62

The seminar took place in Grenoble. Anna und Eugen entered a room furnished with a large table and chairs around it. Older persons and young students, some of them of African origin, were gathered, welcoming Anna joyfully who introduced her English-speaking guest.

Anna: „My friends, before we turn to Aristotelian ethics again, tell me please why you come here and why you delve into antique philosophy. Eugen, our guest, asked me why one should philosophize. Aristotle, by the way, discussed this question with his friend Themison. And here is it written down.

She held up a booklet titled *Protrepticos* and put it aside.“

Anna: „Now please tell us what brings you here.“

Rachid arrived, late as always, and put down his leather jacket, crash helmet and sunglasses. The round was complete.

They struggled as they tried to articulate their thoughts in English, but they helped each other, joked and giggled and got along.

Pierre: „Aristotle is a fascinating type – he explains the world and he teaches me how to think. I want to think like he does. Sharp.“

Amelie: „Yes, but it is strange. He talks about *bliss*. Why this dusty term? He is no mystic or cokehead.

But then he defines precisely what he means using terms like *activity of the soul according to reason* and speaks of bodily and spiritual goods and of practical and of theoretical ways of life, and of various virtues and justice.

At first it sounds like Chinese to me and I must translate it word for word into my own language. Only then, slowly, slowly, I realize: it's brilliant. And – though it is 2500 years old – it's up to date."

Mokhtar: „Yes, brilliant he is and so different, so profound. No hype, no show, no frills. That's what I like."

Marie: „I like that, too. But he is puzzling me all the time. What does he mean by *soul?* He is a scientist, not a theologian. Does he mean *psyche* or *intellect* or what? So I read and think and search and then I discover beautiful things."

Eugen: „Beautiful things?"

Marie: „Oh yes, lots. Important thoughts, if you know what I mean."

Michelle: „Why I come here, you want to know? I want to learn what is good and bad and what to do. People often do what they like and do bad things. But what is good nowadays? The law tells me what is not good. So, I want to read Kant, the philosopher. But Aristotle comes first. Now you know."

Rashid: „I joined a gang and did bad things. Went to jail. Had time to think. Thought I was stupid. Wondered why. Then I came here.

Anna told me, I was looking for a simple recipe. Told me there was no such thing. She showed me how to use my brain. Hey, man, that did it. They won't lock me up again."

Anna applauded: „You were great. Thanks, my friends."

She continued the seminar while Eugen looked on with an air of bewilderment. Then she closed:

„Next week we will talk about *Ibn Sina*. This is what the philosopher Avicenna was called a thousand years ago in his home town Bukhara on the Silk Road. This Islamic scholar had the best brain of his time. He translated some of Aristotle's scriptures into Arabic, thus saving them for us. We owe him a lot."

63

Anna picked an old bar to discuss the seminar. Eugen saw the stucco decoration on the ceiling, the many lamp shades of colored glass and the long rows of bottles before mirrors. Enameled sign-plates on the walls reminded the guests what their parents used to smoke and drink. But he remained unimpressed, since the seminar had not helped him a bit. The group had not dealt with what he perceived to be his problem. It voiced feelings and opinions, but no facts. He still had no idea what could have caused his bot to say: *Protrepticos is beautiful*.

Since Eugen complained to Anna in an agitated manner, curious participants of the seminar surrounded them and listened.

Amelie: „Ah, beauty is the problem. That's what it is, isn't it?"

Eugen: „Aristotle's writings are beautiful. That's what you said. But why is it beautiful? Show me. Prove it. I bet you can't."

This attack stunned, but did not frighten them, least of all the ladies.

Amelie: „Prove beauty? You must be crazy. I know what's beautiful. That's it. Love is beautiful. Why prove it? Ha."

She put an arm around Eugen's neck and kissed him and they all laughed.

Marie: „I guess, Monsieur Eugen is looking for a formula to determine beauty. If a box is one meter long and half a meter wide, symmetrical and shimmering gold, then it is beautiful. Ha."

Again they all laughed. But Eugen agreed: a formula his bot could compute would solve his problem indeed. Michelle, however, called this idea *drôle*, truly funny, and made fun of him again:

„Then, a formula is needed. But why? Show me. Prove it. I bet you can't."

As they all laughed at Eugen, whose glass tipped over, Amelie took his hand and comforted him:

„How amusing this meeting was – philosophy at the counter. I hope, you will come and see us again. For now: *Bon Courage*."

64

Anna chose a scenic route for the way home. Though the Drôme was so very blessed with the beauties of nature, tourists were rather attracted by the High Alps, the Mediterranean and the mighty Roman ruins further south. She drove down the Gorge of the Bourne, rated *worth a voyage.* Neither the sky above nor the river in the valley were to be seen from the road, hewn into the rock, and its many tunnels. Midway through they parked and viewed the scenery. Eugen envied the sweating cyclists who experienced this wonder of nature so very closely:

„How beautiful. Grandiose."

„Oh, a miracle. A bot and his master both talk about beauty. Ha."

They laughed and went on, down the gorge, passed the villages at the foothills and went up again the remote *Col du Pionier* (Pass of the Pioneer), then stopped and savored the wide view of the country.

Anna mused. Obviously, Eugen liked her home and the countryside. But where did he come from? She knew so little about him.

65

„You once told me about the beginnings of Artificial Intelligence, when your work began. Expert systems, you said, should solve hard problems and even surpass humans. Do you remember?"

„Of course I remember the drama playing in the west, the delusions of grandeur and the ventures into a new world of computing. The Americans dreamed of automated offices, the Germans of automated factories. And I recall how the hype and the fraud and the gold rush, went by."

„Why did it go by?"

„People pursued one approach only, hunted for the stronger logic and the faster calculus. In other words, they believed in machine power, favoring a strategy of *brute force.* "

„Why did they do it?"

"This strategy seemed plausible: the strongest rocket reaches the moon, the biggest submarine decides the war and the fastest computer wins the chess championship. *The more the better*, nobody voiced this slogan in public, but they all believed in it. Anna, they were on the wrong track, moving down a gorge as if on rails, unable to brake or turn."

„And how did you fare?"

„I was lucky, which I owed to the Soviet system. Our computers were not good enough and I suspected they never would be. So I thought of a way out: I didn't bet on muscle but on brains, and I will tell you more about it if you wish."

Eugen looked to the distant valley of the Bourne, thinking of Anna. This amazing woman had taken him to her seminar and let him learn about the love of philosophy. She cared for him, no doubt.

„Anna, come with me to Bukhara. I know this ancient town and like it, and you will like it too."

„Bukhara? It would be wonderful." She smiled.

66

Chuck didn't belong to one of the mammoth organizations built to ensure the safety of the USA. He worked in a small elite institute concerned with strategic issues of security. A similar institute had become famous decades ago, devising the means of communication which could survive a nuclear attack. It broke with the tradition of streaming information down a line then switching it to another line, thus letting it zigzag towards its destiny. Such connections were vulnerable, long connections in particular. The new scheme did away with them altogether and the precursor of the Internet was born.

Chuck's team analyzed the inherent threats and weaknesses of the nation's financial system, energy system, medical system and transport system. In recent times a new task came into focus: assessing the threats induced by the networks of the future. They were expected to spread much faster and more pervasively than today's Internet.

Chuck's think-tank and lobby was well financed, well shielded from public interest and well connected. It was located close to Congress and the White House.

The bots hacked the CIA. Wow. They delivered top secret information. Wow. Chuck thought as he drove back from the meeting with Rachel at Bill's house. This he had not anticipated, not in his wildest dreams. He was deeply impressed.

If he had only bots at his disposal, he would have used them at once. An informant inside the *NSA* told him about an investigation code-named *Chimera*. The *NSA* did not know what it had come across. It only knew that strange data pervaded the Internet – neither text nor audio nor video. All attempts to decode the data had failed and no patterns of movement could be recognized. Perhaps an unknown dysfunction of the network had caused the phenomenon. But the *NSA* would not accept anything unknown occurring on the Internet – the realm it ruled.

Had the NSA traced Rachel's bots? Chuck pondered. Bots would find out about this in secret.

67

Rachel, Betty and Joe, Vijay and Bill gathered in Chuck's office of steel and glass and reviewed the past year: Eugen's failure, Rachel's risk and Vijay's rescue.

Chuck: „This drama, my friends, would have been much less dramatic, had the bots not performed so extraordinarily well. But that's in the past. Let's look ahead now. Bot technology must not lie idle – it is more important than ever."

Vijay: „But you know what happened."

Chuck: „I received alarming news: the terror scene is changing. Religious fanatics and terrorist cells are dropping out and the big boys are taking over, those who deal with drugs and prostitution and laundered money, very big money that is, around the globe.

These guys know how to scare everyone: governments, big business and the clergy. Tactical nukes, guided missiles, cyberwar technologies – you name it, they got it."

Rachel: „The Security Council discussed this topic three years ago."

Chuck: „Yes, we have foreseen it. But we didn't foresee it would happen so fast. There must be top brains at work. And they soon will show us what they are up to. Too bad, we have no idea who they are and what they will do next.

Now you will understand my message: *We need bots. And that's your job*."

They interrupted the session discussing Chuck's plea, while he prepared a video presentation.

Then they saw the Berlin Congress Center where the annual Chaos Computer Convention (*CCC*), the Hacker Olympics, took place. Jean and Wacko appeared.

Chuck: „The one with the jacket is Jean. French. Great guy. Discovered Eugen for us. The one with the tattoo is Wacko. German. Wacky. Founded the *Deluge Archeology Network*. But see for yourself."

Wacko stepped to the speaker's desk, fins and snorkel in hand, the symbols of surviving a deluge. Addressing an audience of Europeans, Chinese, Indians and Middle Easterners, he didn't give a damn for manners, but entertained the crowd splendidly, telling jokes and showing a photo of himself dressed in sheepskin splitting wood – the post-deluge-hero who survives without Internet and central heating.

Then he introduced the *Deluge Archeology Network*, populated by 2.000 computer nerds, the *Archos*. Raising his arms high above his head he called for solidarity among all computer wizards of the earth to fight the deluges to come. At last he closed by singing the Archo Anthem using the melody of the Internationale:

Es rettet uns kein höh'res Wesen,
kein Gott, kein Kaiser noch Tribun.
Uns von der Sintflut zu erlösen
können wir nur selber tun!

[*No higher creature will us save / no god or tribune down will delve / to shield us from deluge's wave. / We got to do it ourselves!*]

As Wacko began to sing, all the Archos in the room jumped to their feet, sang along and applauded frenetically. Betty applauded, too:

„What an evangelist. Awesome. Killer. Will win a million followers."

Chuck stopped the video.

Rachel: „It's the latest fad. They are looking for computers which became conspicuous during the deluge – via crashes and dumps, irregular backups and the like. They hope to find remnants they can analyze. It's catching on like wildfire."

Vijay laughed:

„Silly nitwits, scratching and scrabbling, and gaggling when they find what puzzles them. But you cannot find a bot, neither arm nor leg, nor eye nor ear. There is no archeology. Let's go home."

But Chuck pulled the breaks:

„Nobody knows anything with certainty. Not even you, Vijay. Parts of bots may still be out there, perhaps even a functioning bot. And what if some genius deciphers it.

„Nonsense. So, what do you propose?"

„I propose bots as you may guess. Vijay, it probably never occurred to you: your deluge, was the biggest hacking-event of the decade. A show in blazing colors. Face it: You made every hacker chomp at the bit. Need I say more?"

Betty: „Forget that. I know why Eugen went bonkers. I was on the verge of it myself."

Chuck: „I don't worry about Eugen, he will be alright. I worry about you. Get your butts on the line. You hear me? Damn it. Get going and deliver!"

The team didn't look at Chuck and didn't comment. Only Bill looked at Chuck, trying to read his mind and he saw Chuck's fear of Terry. Then he looked at the faces of the team and what he saw made him doubtful.

Vijay had killed the bots off with pleasure. Would he build new and better bots for Chuck, more mercenaries? Bill didn't count on Vijay.

And Betty, the perfectionist who was so close to Eugen? Perhaps she knew enough about bots to remove their most dangerous features. But would she deliver cripples? Probably not. Rachel, finally, had been terribly burned by the risks she had taken. Would she take another risk she could not calculate? Probably not. And Eugen? He had not mentioned bots once during Bill's calls. He seemed entirely detached and absorbed by other things.

Bill realized, nobody was holding the team together, Chuck least of all. The team's power was gone and the project a pile of shards. This was the bitter truth.

Finally, Chuck closed the meeting without a solution. He accompanied the team to the elevator and wished it farewell. As they were about to part on the street, Rachel paused:

„My friends, never before have I been part of a project as exciting as ours. I don't know how you feel, now that it dies. No, I don't think we will deliver. But let's get together one last time and bury the project in style. Let's meet again in Arizona."

But Joe raised his hands.

„Have pity! Not the desert! Washington is bad enough for an old man. Come to VeniceBeach, come to visit me. But don't come without plan.

Think about what you'd love to do more than anything else. Only if you are clear about it, come to Venice Beach. And bring your swimsuits.

I will fly home now. Fare thee well, my friends."

He hailed a cab and was gone.

68

As always in autumn, Anna's garden looked a little disorderly. Weeds grew on harvested beds and scrub in the greenhouses. The tendrils of the brambles had grown to full length, also the shoots of zucchini and pumpkin. Leaves and stems of beets and peas and flowers intertwined.

Eugen was sitting on the bench next to the old fountain looking on the garden's plenty of plants and fruit. Kittens were playing with balls of string at his feet. Anna approached, putting a basket down – her harvest of the day. Then she went to fetch the mail, letters and a journal, and sat down besides Eugen. Both liked the spot's peaceful charm at the zenith of the gardening year.

Anna picked the journal and studied its flashy cover: A waterfall was gushing into a network of pipes, bloating and ripping them apart. This network, it seemed, could explode any moment. The title read: *Who Caused the Deluge?* Anna passed the paper on to Eugen.

„Voilà. The hunt is on."

Eugen leafed through the journal and threw it down scornfully.

„True, a thousand hunters are underway but none of them will catch anything."

Eugen handed Anna some sheets of paper.

„Look, more images without words. My bot sent them."

Both looked at a jumble of things: flowers, blossoms and fruit. They were regularly shaped, in contrast to the wing of a bat, a maple tree in winter, and a leaf.

Anna: „Fascinating. See the veins of the wing and the veins of the leaf and the branches and twigs on the tree. How delicate they are – branching out to the end." Then they looked at spirals of many sorts: a galaxy and a snail shell. Anna spread the images on the ground:

„It's strange. Before, your bot sent you manmade things, simple artifacts, geometric figures. Now this: Natural things. It seems the bot is growing up."

Eugen laughed:

„Like a child, you mean?"

Again they studied the strange collection. All images were beautiful in their own way. But Eugen could not make sense of them:

„O.k. Beautiful they may be. But what is the virtue of beauty, as you philosophers would put it?"

„I guess, something is beautiful if it is sound and intact. Beauty is a sign of life and hope."

She took a ripe apple from the basket and put it in Eugen's lap.

„Look. It is beautiful, sound and wholesome. Eat it."

Anna left. Eugen took a bite and began to think back to the long days he spent at the clinic. He remembered the booklet of an architect which struck him after leafing through dozens of books in the little library. Its images of a Bedouin tent, a car, a bridge and a pylon had mesmerized him instantly and slowly he had recognized their beauty. The images had been soothing every time he looked at them. But why?

Relaxed, Eugen viewed the so very familiar garden. Yet he wondered. He saw ever more detail, ever new images. Images! They seemed powerful.

He had suffered a nervous breakdown, the doctors had told him, a stress syndrome, probably caused by overload, burnout. They had examined his brain, but found no signs of a stroke or epileptic disorder. His senses worked well for his age. Thus, his doctors' diagnoses remained as nebulous as his own diagnosis of his bot.

Eugen admitted that he had become a little cranky. He remembered colleagues who became quite odd long before they retired. And he would not exclude the possibility that his bot had turned cranky as well.

69

Since 1960 the USSR and Cyprus stayed on very friendly terms. Many Russians lived on the island enjoying the Mediterranean climate, privacy and banks well connected to the east and west. Here, one lived an unhurried life, easy and cheap.

Pjotr lived here at times; and like most Russians he possessed a Cypriot passport, a house and a company with a branch in London.

In the garden, enclosed by a wall, four persons were sitting around a table: Pjotr, Alam, and two plainly clad women, Lyudmila und Lydia, Pjotr's top staff. All were staring at notebooks, busy with Alam's order. Alam demonstrated the details of a municipal communications network.

„Here is the core zone, there the power supply, at the left are the gateways and switches of the police;

next the private hubs of the medical center, right the servers of the National Guard. And over there the old mainframes for the administration of water, power and public affairs."

Pjotr judged the order and said jokingly:

„Well, I guess, I can't refuse."

Alam sent him a cutting glance. Jokes were inappropriate now. This was dead serious. Then, the women announced the result of their calculations.

„176 servers, 57 routers, 19 switches, 16 mainframes. It's manageable, except for the mainframes. They are ancient. All in all two months lead time. Error rate 15%."

Alam: "No errors, Pjotr! You understand me? Take your best men."

Pjotr pointed to Lydia and Lyudmila:

„My best men are these ladies. Trust me, we will do a perfect job. It's in our interest. If we botch it, we are all dead."

„Well-paid and dead."

They rose, the men embraced the oriental way and Alam left.

Pjotr, Lyudmila and Lydia passed the cognac bottle, upbeat and drinking to their entry into big business.

„You will be rich, my little doves, very rich. We would have had to spend years in the banking business to earn half the dough. Now we will get there in a few months."

Lyudmila: „These old mainframes are worrying me. Ancient software, hardware even older, and not linked to the Internet, accessible only via an old switch. I will have to blow up one of them, just to make sure things work.

161

Lydia: „Take it easy. If we don't take these clunkers out, no one will notice in the chaos."

Pjotr: „You think the mainframes haven't been hacked in the deluge?"

Lyudmila: „I'll find out."

Pjotr: „What do we know about the technologies used in the deluge?"

Lydia: „We know nothing, nothing at all. Just like Wacko und his Archos. If they knew anything the net overloaded. Still we should keep an eye on him."

Pjotr: „You bet I will. I'd prefer Eugen, however. But I can't find him. Not yet."

70

Bill, Rachel and Vijay, Betty und Joe gathered in Venice Beach in the shabby little house close to the beach Joe had rented.

When hungry, they ambled over to the *Noodle Factory*, a restaurant favored by surfers who lunched in T-shirts, shorts and sandals. The team plunged into this carefree ambience right away and after the first cocktail, Washington, Boston und Stanford seemed to lie on a different continent.

Joe called the waitress *honey*, kissed her cheek and told stories:

"Over there, a very big wave stripped a girl naked. Proud and beautiful as a goddess, she came to the beach in the morning sun, and smiled at me. That's Venice, the greatest place on earth."

Later he told them how he met Betty in the heydays of Artificial Intelligence. He and his team were out to program the ultimate knowledge machine – inspired by the theory Betty had published.

„Betty warned us and said this nut was too hard to crack for us. Of course, we didn't listen, we were gung-ho. And of course we failed and what a joke it was. If we only we had stopped our fancy, our delusions of grandeur. If just for once we had been honest with each other, this mess would not have happened.

My friends, this is what I want to tell you: let's stay honest, then we will do alright. Now, enjoy your dinner."

Joe was the soul of the meeting. He cared a lot for Vijay and Rachel who carried a heavy load – Chuck's ruthless order and Bill's tacit hope that a stroke of genius would save the project and restore his tarnished image.

With Joe acting as the master of ceremonies, they had fun on the beach and in the bars. When they took a break, he played old records – treasures he had dug up in his attic. Sometimes he even read from Kerouac's *On the Road*, the classic of the Beatnik-days and while he was reading his pot-brownies went round like in the good old times of Venice Beach.

Joe, the old man with the young mind, saw to it that they set neither goals nor deadlines. And it was Joe who questioned most radically what he termed the *dogma of the bots*:

„Why the heck should bot technology stay secret? Let's make it public, let's have an *Open Bot*, and let a thousand young geniuses gather behind the bot-idea. Super cool this is."

Betty: „Ah, you are nuts. I can hear the gangsters cheering."

„No, sweetie, think ahead. Open technology is safe technology."

Joe, in fact, gave a damn for bot design - a taboo, since the meeting on the ranch. Now he had broken the spell. Arguments went back and forth in lively discussion:

„Why should bots conquer the entire Internet? Would less not be more?"

„And why must bots act autonomously? People could guide them."

„Should our bots, these lone rangers, not better work in teams?"

„And why not have a variety of specialist bots tailored to market needs?"

Eventually, it came as a surprise to them that they were contesting the purpose of the project, and Joe was pleased:

„Wow. You have come a long way and shed a heavy load. The ghost of the bot haunts you no more. As a team you have reached puberty, my friends. Now you are ready to take the next step.

Let me hear what motivates you, what motivates you deep inside. Come over and sit down in a circle."

As they sat around a bottle of Southern Comfort, Joe addressed Betty:

„Want to start?"

Betty: „The inevitable happened: Eugen and his bots fell victim to *Gödel's Curse*."

The Curse, that's how she called the famous proof by the logician Karl Gödel: Every formal theory is contradictory and thus inconsistent, if only it is sufficiently complex. Complexity thus may ruin a theory. And it may have thwarted their attempt to build a bot.

„It worries me my friends, it's killing me. Imagine I built a *Strange Loop* into the bot, overlooked a self-reference. It's easy to walk into this trap which is all but obvious."

Betty showed the screen of her notebook. On display was M. C. Escher's image *Drawing Hands* where the right hand is drawing the left hand which in turn is drawing the right hand. Here things were going round in an endless strange loop: Each hand draws the other and together they are drawing themselves.

"Why, only why was the bot not able to stop thinking about itself?

Some of you may know that Eugen had a soft spot for the *Society of Mind* which may cause the bot's misbehavior. Via a kind of bourse, all components can talk to each other. It is an elegant and democratic mechanism. Everyone may speak up any time and be heard. But unfortunately anyone is allowed to talk till the cows come home and keep the bot busy.

I am looking into this. Hey, I want to break Gödel's Curse or die."

Vijay: „Betty, this may interest you."

He told the astonished team that Eugen released one bot into freedom. This bot then sent back images of *beautiful things*, thus baffling Eugen: why on earth was the bot interested in something for which he was not programmed?

Betty: „Ha. Beauty and the Beast. Very interesting. The bot puzzles me, too. Sometimes it does something surprising, and I cannot find a reason why it did so and how. These surprises seem to emerge by themselves, like ant hills."

They discussed the miracle of ant hills. No ant knows anything about an ant hill, and no construction plan exists. The hill must somehow be in the genes of ants: thousands of them touch and smell each other and do little things. Lo and behold, an ant hill emerges practically by itself.

Betty: „I have looked for such phenomena in bots, but haven't found anything yet. Still, I believe something unknown resides in bots."

Joe: „Oh come on. You know every single line of bot-code."

„Believe me I am serious: something seems to emerge when thousands of components interact like ants. Now this bot's sense of beauty gives me a lead and I'll give it a shot."

71

Bill was listening quietly as always and wondering what occupied people's minds. Betty seemed to love the toughest challenges she could find. She was strangely extreme. He himself was not as radical by far as the ladies, Rachel and Betty.

Rachel and Betty could not have been more diverse, however. Ever since Bill had lured Rachel into his team, she had been thinking of her kin in Tel Aviv – mother, sister, nephews – and, therefore, doing the utmost for the project. She suffered from the worry of not doing enough. After all she witnessed the growing dangers in the Middle East day by day.

Even before the team had met on the ranch, Rachel was inclined to build a device similar to a bot, but without frills. She did not care about Russia, India and

China. Her device should move to places like Teheran, Beirut and Damascus. It would be simple, bread-and-butter technology only, and humans would control it. This she had told Bill on the ranch after she cursed Eugen, who opposed the course she had wanted to take.

In Venice she didn't say a word about her old plans. She thanked Vijay cordially for his help, said how shocked she still was by the enormity of the deluge, and announced her plans to resume the research she had done before the project. In fact, she was looking forward to it because the testing ground for bots – this unique miniature replica of the Internet – allowed her to study innovations no one else could.

Bill wondered whether Rachel had given up on bots altogether. Had she secretly progressed? He listened carefully when Rachel named the functions she considered dead weight and proposed to discard: bots need not replicate nor act on their own accord. He remembered her saying a bot should be designed like a virtual drone, a device one could direct to a specific target in the net, in order to spy on it or destroy it.

Bill assumed if Rachel was working on virtual drones, she had not yet reached her goal. She would probably need Betty to stabilize a bot's cognitive apparatus, the part of software Rachel would not touch.

Joe: „Thanks Betty. You let us know where your heart beats. You never take the easy way out. Thus, the best of luck from all of us. And tell us when the bot works. Who is next?"

It was Vijay's turn. Vijay:

„My heart does not beat for bots. I happily eradicated these beasts in spite of the billion-dollar damage done. But what now? Shouldn't we strengthen our defenses against bots? It would make sense if Chuck is right, that the cyber mob will strike quite soon. But bot defense must function nationwide and, thus, needs a very big effort."

Bill expected this kind of comment, which sounded reasonable, but revealed nothing about Vijay's desires. Bill recalled the meeting at Stanford where Vijay had confided that he was afraid: he had skirted his father's question how he served peace and the harmony of mankind. His father, a wise and shrewd and strict man would certainly find that bots could be misused and end up in the hands of criminals. His father would not approve of him being at work with bots.

Bill: „You would be bored by bot-defense, would you not?"

Vijay didn't answer. Instead he began to talk about mechanisms of life which could be modeled and simulated in a computer. His replication-model of algae was an instance in case.

Vijay: „This model is a tiny step to something bigger, called *Artificial Life.*"

He ascribed enormous potential to this scientific discipline. Eventually, it would allow to model and study not only individual mechanisms like replication, but entire organisms. And once artificial organisms existed in computers, it was possible to analyze small groups and large populations of them. Such deep models could explain all social phenomena causally, rendering statistics obsolete.

Bill: „You are interested in humans, not machines?"

Vijay: „I am interested in societies – artificial societies for now and human societies later on."

„So, you start by modeling its members?"

„And I hope my dream comes true, which is to
learn what causes harmony and what destroys it.

Never before had Vijay spoken with such candor,
revealing his vision and fascinating his listeners. Joe
jumped up:

„Kick-ass. You were wonderful – opened your
hearts just the way I had hoped for. I need a break now:
I have to digest this load of information. So, go for a
walk my friends, go swimming and look at the dancers.
Tomorrow at ten we meet again. Until then, have fun."

All of them needed a break, but felt they had
reached closure. In only a few days, their attention had
shifted away from the project's technologies and challenges. Now it was dawning on them that there was
more: things hiding in the background, but running in
their blood.

As they gathered again, they knew, Eugen strived
for perfect intelligence, Vijay for perfect harmony and
Rachel for perfect security. This seemed the real reason
why the project had crumbled.

72

„Hey Joe, you haven't said anything yet. It's your turn
now. What is it you are after?"

While working on bots in the Skunk Works, Joe
had despaired in view of the myriad of possibilities of
adjusting a bot.

„I'd rather tune my car's carburetor by hand,
which is difficult enough, than tune a bot. There are

hundreds of parameters which make tuning bots like gambling. The outcome is unpredictable and I hate it."

Therefore, Joe dreamed of a computer game where bot-armies fought each other. The game could be played until the best army remained undefeated, thus winning a prize.

Thousands of players, could have fun molding and trimming bots and testing them, by letting them fight. Of course they would be toy-bots – fenced-in on Rachel's server-farm.

"Believe me, this game, *World of Botcraft*, will eclipse all other games. Bill you will forget about chess. You can spy on your enemy, play tricks and cheat, and you are going to be young again.

When we finally learn how to tune a winning bot, we will have learned more about bots than ever before. So, Bill, don't forget to fork over the prize money, $10.000."

What a fancy idea – they applauded Joe. Then they paused, having come to the end.

Bill: "Thanks, Joe, we owe you a lot. You brought us here. You guided us, with a firm hand. All of us spoke, all of us listened, and all of us understood. Thus, we achieved closure and are happy about it. We can go home now. Joe, we wish you well. Take care."

They left. Rachel und Vijay went on to Los Angeles, where a conference was to deal with a hot topic: the Internet Deluge.

73

The Biltmore Hotel preserved the splendor, elegance and charm of the nineteen-twenties. Carpets, lounges, paintings, cut-glass cabinets, crystal chandeliers, aureate faucets in luxury suites reminded of grand old times. This hotel hosted the *Internet Deluge Conference.*

It was designed to be a small, intimate, and interactive and creative get-together. Professors, officials and hackers, Americans, Europeans and Asians could get in touch. Since the press had hyped speculations about the deluge and politics tried to shape the public opinion, the time had come to consider matters more soberly and seriously.

Some 250 participants flocked to the conference venue. Vijay und Rachel had coffee while watching the crowd. Rachel whispered to Vijay:

„You must be proud. Without you, nothing would be happening here.“

Men of displeasing appearance caught their attention. Vijay:

„What brings these gentlemen up to town?“

„Hacking 3.0. The fast buck.“

They entered the grand auditorium where Odile, the elegant professor from Grenoble, gave an invited talk. She referred to the deluge's violent effects on the French section of the Internet and the French economy. And she reported of the precautions taken recently to mitigate, if not block out a second deluge. She talked of sensors, filters, monitors, mirrors, redundancies and strategies of network management. An optimistic outlook ended the speech and the audience applauded politely. Then she opened the discussion and Wacko, complete with neck tattoo took to the floor microphone:

„You tell us nothing can explain the deluge. Right you are. And this is the very reason why we will face another deluge. It will take out your precautions and wash them away, professor."

The audience murmured approvingly and some whistled as Wacko went on:

„A computer crashed during the deluge, saving information for a restart. Thus we found strange code – exotic and highly interesting. We are still learning from it.

I therefore urge you, professor, scrutinize the entire French network! Find similar fossils! Collect and share them! We must all learn from them."

The audience applauded spontaneously. Pjotr, wearing a facial mask, had listened, too. Now he used his mobile phone and left the room.

Rachel: „Did the German find anything? What do you think?"

Vijay: „This I don't know. I only know he is risking his tattooed neck."

74

Eugen, still fiddling with the bot, turned to the question: *What is beauty?* If he understood the essence of beauty he might better understand the nature of the bot, so he hoped. Books about design, fashion, art and geometry piled up on the floor of his studio. All images his bot ever sent him were pinned on a wall – a dodecahedra next to a marguerite's blossom, the wings of a butterfly and a snail shell. Below a galaxy hung next to a maple leaf, a starfish, a pyramid and more. Anna entered and once again studied the collection of objects

Eugen: „I am not getting anywhere. Just treading water.

Obviously Eugen was struggling. He felt he was denied to strike the last chord after having played a concert. He had been close, so very close to accomplishing his theory, his life's work.

Anna: „Your bot sends images without any explanation?"

„True. He doesn't communicate the way we do. He is not blessed with social skills. He doesn't need that."

„So, he is more cat than dog."

„He is an autistic cat. Ha. Bots don't cooperate. It would be too risky and much too complex. He has no friends. Whom should he talk to?"

„But he wrote you: *Beautiful*."

„True, this he wrote. But did he write it for me? My mother's cat often laid a dead mouse at the doorstep. We loved the cat and the cat liked us too, but we didn't know whether the cat wanted to give us a present or tell us something. Perhaps it simply put it down, preferring my mother's food to the taste of mice. So, who knows what *beautiful* means to him, if it means anything."

„Does your bot have feelings?"

„I could implant feelings, virtual feelings, but I didn't do it. Why should I?"

Anna was sitting on the floor, eyes closed. Then she looked to the images on the wall – slowly, one by one. She looked at them the way a bot would look at them, without emotion. She caught herself liking the image of a flower for its sunny warm colors and a butterfly for its tender light colors. For the bot, she supposed, such beauty would be meaningless. He also would not notice if an image appeared peppy or dull, delicate or cloddy.

Anna tried to imagine a bot that never went for a walk and was never enchanted by the landscape around him, a bot which never watched the stars in the sky and merely scanned files in computer archives. Her imagination gave out.

Anna knew she somehow had to mask her feelings and she tried it by masking all color and content and meaning of images: she concentrated on form only and on geometry. This exercise felt like fasting and meditating and her brain emptied. Then the forms began to appeal to her and concepts entered her thinking: *proportion, regularity, symmetry, harmony*.

She quickly rose.

„Eugen, the riddle's solution is staring at us. Your bot found absolute beauty: The Golden Section, the Divine Proportion, and Phi, which they call the *Number of Life*. And perhaps he dances with joy."

„So, this is it?"

Slowly Eugen became aware that Phi dominated all objects on the wall. Even the spiraling arms of a galaxy grew according to the Golden Section, which seemed ingrained in nature. Eugen groaned:

„Aaaah. It is a number after all. Beauty is a number. And my bot found it."

He hugged Anna and was relieved for a moment. Then his mind went into overdrive. If Phi was the solution, where did it hide inside the bot? And how could he have found it? Phi stood for the simple formula: $a / b = (a + b) / a$. Of course his bot had no problem computing it. But why did he deem it special?

„Anna, tell me, why is Phi beautiful?"

„Nonsense. Not the number is beautiful. Only the form of things can be beautiful. And don't ask why. Remember what Amelie told you in the old bar."

Eugen remembered well: *Prove beauty? You are nuts. I know what's beautiful. That's it.*

Again Eugen hugged Anna. This astounding woman had given him so much since they first talked about the mysterious kalós kai agathós.

„Anna, today is a great day. I gained hope again after a long time. You gave me hope. What a wonderful present it is. I thank you my dear."

75

Wacko was kidnapped in Los Angeles. In a luxurious trailer he was strapped on a bed, naked. The hair on his left temple had been shaved and an injection device prepared. A car approached and parked. Pjotr stepped out and entered the trailer.

Pjotr: „Guten Tag mein Herr. Wie geht es Ihnen?" [*Good day sir. How are you?*]

Unstrapped, Wacko had to sit on the rim of the bed, and a woman sprayed on his back and took a syringe.

„Relax now. Stay calm. Now don't move."

Wacko received an injection into his spine. Then a little object was injected under the skin of his temple, the bleeding stopped and the wound glued shut.

After this routine treatment, Wacko was clad in a bath robe and offered a Coke.

Pjotr: „The implant is quite effective. I guess we can talk now. Let's talk about my favorite topic: the penetration of computers."

76

Since the deluge, Wacko had belonged to the group of surveilled persons, whose activities Chuck wanted to know about. Now all contacts to Wacko were broken. He had not given his talk at the conference nor had he spent the night at the hotel, and his mobile was dead. His last message, which said he was in contact with Russians, alarmed Chuck.

Cyber-gangsters had probably traced the Archos for some time. Jean's seminal paper and Wacko's allusions in Berlin had alerted them and now they were waiting in the wings. They would grab Wacko, grill him, and in the end abduct or ditch him.

After that they would kidnap Jean and learn about Eugen. Both were in serious danger – perhaps by Russians. Bill promised to warn them immediately and it was all he could do.

77

Anna and Eugen were flying across the Uzbek Steppe towards Bukhara the town, which had been old when its greatest son, Ibn Sina, researched, taught and cured there, a thousand years ago. Eugen had visited the town to hire a physicist for his institute.

„We were young and liked each other. After she showed me the town, she introduced me to her father Alim who prayed five times a day even in Soviet times. I remember him well: One evening he asked me about god and I spoke my mind: *There may be a god, but there is nothing we can know about god with certainty.* He looked at me intensely, then shook his head in disbelief, smiling kindly. Then he served strong sweet tea and started a conversation about our faiths which lasted throughout the night. I didn't convince him and he didn't convert me. Yet he introduced me to the grand culture and violent history of Bukhara which means *Site of Luck.* It was a wonderful time, and so will it be again, Anna."

Anna, too, thought of happy times, when she had moved to Paris for her first job at the Sorbonne. The vaults of this university stored copies and translations of the works of Aristotle. Some of them, like the books on Physics and Metaphysics, would have been lost forever, had not a handful of Islamic scholars translated them into Arabic. One of them, Ibn Sina, deemed philosophy the *art of arts*, and Aristotle's philosophy the treasure of western wisdom.

Aristotle's writings at the Sorbonne attracted scientists for long, among them Aristotle's most famous fan, Thomas Aquinas. In the 13th century he travelled all the way from southern Italy to Paris.

Anna: „I met Carl, an American, who studied the parchments of Avicenna, as Ibn Sina was called by his Latin name. Carl specialized in the zenith of Islamic erudition at the turn of the millennium and he opened my mind for it. What a wonderful time it was. It makes my heart leap."

They approached towers and shining blue domes, then the small aircraft landed. Later they strolled through the city and rested in a sidewalk café. Anna pointed to a mosque close by:

„It has seen wanderers between Europe and China, caravans loaded with treasures and adventurers underway for years."

„And here Ibn Sina studied Aristotle, I suppose."

„Oh no, when this old mosque was built, Ibn Sina must have been dead for 500 years."

„What a man …"

„… who helped Europe leave the Middle Ages behind."

„You revere him?"

„Of course I do. Ibn Sina is a superstar."

While they were talking, a traditionally-clad man walked by. When he heard the name *Ibn Sina* he stopped and turned to them. Smiling he repeated the philosopher's name and spoke to them in his Uzbek language. Aware that they could not communicate, he laughed, slowly ambling on.

Eugen: „It seems Ibn Sina remained a star in east and west."

The next day, Anna and Eugen visited a mosque and, sitting on the carpet on the floor, marveled at the finery and harmony of the tiled walls, columns, balustrades and cupolas around them.

Eugen: „This place soothes body and soul – like Bach's music."

„It is a symphony in Phi. Ha."

They let their minds sweep and with time the filigree decor and the endless detail mesmerized them fully.

Eugen also thought of the rough times Alim had told him about. When the mosque was built the horse people of Central Asia were in uproar. How was it possible that these people created perfect beauty nonetheless? Then his thoughts wandered back to the cruel times when the Abbey Saint Antoine was built. It seemed to him, that war and misery, faith and beauty belonged together. Then his bot came to mind.

„Anna, don't laugh at me. I had a strange thought. When picturing my bot, I used to imagine *him* – the cunning warrior. Now I am beginning to see *her*, the keeper of beauty. And I am certain she would love to join us here in this beautiful place."

Anna paused. She was flabbergasted.

„I can't believe it. Hey, you permitted yourself to think totally out of the box. That's something else. Man, you are getting along. No, I am not laughing at you. I am smiling."

Anna was convinced the bot would progress like her maker. She was Eugen's brainchild and eventually she would do what Rachel's bots could not.

Anna strongly felt the mosque's healing spirit, which, no doubt, affected Eugen. She whispered:

„Harmony can heal a bot as well."

78

At home again, Henri welcomed Anna und Eugen with apprehension. He alerted the police, he said. Yesterday they had checked the house and found it burgled. Housebreaking was not uncommon in the vicinity where houses lay dispersed in the hills, inhabited only on weekends. The looters had probably had an easy time; no one had seen them coming or leaving, and the old doors could not keep them out.

Henri had come over to feed the cats and water the garden since it had not rained. Then he had seen the door to the courtyard ajar and a cable lying on the floor. That's when he had entered and looked about. The kitchen seemed untouched, the living room orderly. Only Anna's desk was rummaged through and her computer gone. *These were burglars with manners* Henri thought, until the police had come and revealed the mess in Eugen's studio.

Anna and Eugen found the furniture intact, the books untouched, even the valuable 17th century statue was still in place. Obviously, the thieves were not interested in money. Missing were all computers and storage media.

The damage, thus, had stayed within bounds. Anna would buy a new notebook and retrieve her data form the Internet where she had saved it. Since Eugen's computers were of special design it would take some time to replace them.

Henri: „Eugen, you gave me your old computer. You can have it back."

Eugen was relieved. This machine was crammed with software of great value, and at Henri's it was safely parked.

A glass of wine before them, Anna and Eugen began to calm down in the kitchen and talk things over. The police would find nothing of use. If there was a car involved, it left no trace in the gravel and the whole event was probably only a matter of minutes.

What had been the motive to snatch computers and data? Certainly not the hardware – much better products were on the market. Data? No, Eugen did not store fodder for hackers.

If software was the target then the circle of interested persons shrank dramatically. Only professionals could use it. And probably they did not go for bot software they aimed at the intruder only – a most valuable device to some.

Eugen: „I guess, they hacked us before. And they did find software but could not handle it. This is why they took the whole machine. And now they are analyzing it.

Anna: „We have been hacked?"

„Most likely. That's why they knew we were travelling."

„I am glad we were not at home. Imagine they had broken in by force."

„Criminals who stick at nothing. I know the type."

„Will they come back? I am afraid."

„I am afraid, too. Anna, we are on their radar screen, Jean and I."

79

One forenoon, the shutters of Eugen's studio were still closed, all lamps in the room lit, and the computer screen showing a bot as a hive of pulsating modules.

Observers were somehow attracted by the strange creature which seemed to smile. Eugen had reshaped the skull-like appearance – adapting it to an image he stored in the background of the bot. Thus shimmering through the bot was a smiling face. Whether it was a male or female face one could not tell.

Eugen had fallen asleep on the bed, still fully dressed. He opened the eyes as Anna knocked on the door and entered.

„You spent the night with your bot?"

When Eugen nodded she sat down beside him to learn more. Eugen pointed to the computer.

„She visited me and I looked at her. But I understand her less and less. She is so complex. It's exhausting. She has learned so much and changed a lot."

He closed his eyes, sighed and paused. Then he went on:

„I still don't know anything about her sense of beauty, know nothing of the beauty of Protrepticos. If I only knew."

„Once you told me about ants building a ant-hill while knowing nothing about it. Perhaps her sense of beauty is like an emerging ant-hill. And you should not look for the hill but for the ants. They can lead you to their hill. Eugen and the quest for ants. Ha."

„I will never understand her."

Anna opened the window, filling the room with light and fresh air. Then she pointed to the figure on the screen:

„Oh, come off it. Courage! She is not so strange. She has your genes. And be proud of her. She is a good girl."

Anna caressed Eugen's face and kissed him. Eugen sighed again, utterly relieved, and took Anna in his arms.

Breakfast time was past when Eugen had a last glimpse of the computer and stopped.

„Anna, look here, a message from the bot – cryptic as always – Russian names. They are the names of towns near St Petersburg, ugly places by the way. So, she probably doesn't pursue her beautiful hobby."

„The bot is in the east? Perhaps our computers went east, too, carrying a stowaway?"

„And perhaps she jumped ship looking for beauty."

„Or she remembers her duties as bot. Ha."

Eugen told Anna about the Russian crime scene, how he had run away from it, and about Bill's recent warning and concern: Russians may have kidnapped a friend of Jean's and he feared the worst."

„Heavens. Here, they broke into my house and there they kidnapped and perhaps murdered someone. It's good that your bot lives. Never have I hoped more for her than today."

80

This Sunday the leisurely life in Cyprus had slowed down even more. Pjotr was sleeping in the garden in the shade of a tree. His staff had gone to the beach and taken the dog along. Pjotr wore shorts; newspaper, phone and glasses lay in the grass.

Three men approached via the house: Alam and his bodyguards. Alam surveyed Pjotr's domicile for some time. Now the time had come for a visit.

„Pardon me my friend. I am intruding. But we must be careful. You understand. Let's talk."

They sat down at the table face to face.

Alam: „Time has come. On the 27th at 04:16:25 CET all systems must be dead. Is that clear? Repeat."

Pjotr repeated.

„Well, well. My friend, our double strike will rock the world. You will be proud. And rich. Here is the first installment."

When Alam put the pouch on the table, he recognized concern in Pjotr's face and asked in a menacing tone:

„Any problems, Pjotr?"

„Time is short, damned short."

„Really? But we rely on you. That's all for today. Good evening, Pjotr."

Piotr's hands were shaking as he pulled a small jewel case from the pouch and opened it. When he saw diamonds of the best quality his worried look changed to a smile. Entering the new market had already paid off.

81

Eugen was sitting in his favorite spot in the garden, on the bench near the fountain, feet put up. He looked at the notebook on his lap and the endless stream of data flowing across the screen. Now and then he inspected what had arrived: files of all sorts, newspaper clippings, dossiers, faxes, photographs, voice recordings, videos, tables and records and more. When Anna came up to him, he put his headphones down.

Anna: „What an idyllic sight: A Russian hero at work."

„Alright, I am taking it easy, twiddling my thumbs. But my bot, the good girl, is working her butt off. She is the true heroine. Come, sit next to me. I want to show you some pictures."

From the list of file names, some of them in Cyrillic and Arabic script, he activated a video taken by the surveillance camera of the Green Hall in St. Petersburg.

„Look here, it's Pjotr, our particular friend. We may owe the burglary to him."

„Oh, grand robes, Champagne and caviar. Fine folk in a wonderful hall. What's going on?"

„I am working on it, checking related files: voice messages, emails and faxes. Now you see Aleksander, a well-connected eminence grise. I know him well, he is probably hosting the venue. Now he introduces Pjotr to a Middle Eastern looking man. We will soon know who he is. Oh, they are talking intently – seem to have common interests."

„Pjotr looks like he has a lot on his record."

„This he has indeed. And the world will soon know about it."

„What are you going to do?"

„Three day after tomorrow you will hear and see it on the news."

„She is still sending you stuff. Lots of it."

„Now she is sending stuff from the Chamber of Commerce and the Agency of Foreign Trade. Then she will search the Secret Service of the Interior and the police. After that she will scan Pjotr's machines a second time hunting for hidden links. And in due course she will take interest in Pjotr's *friends*.

It will take a little while, but she knows her craft well. I taught her."

82

A small grey bus, its windows trellised, stopped on the sidewalk, and a squad of armed policemen were rushing from it into an office building and up the stairs. The splintering of a door was heard and soon after a file of handcuffed men and women came down the stairs and were escorted to the bus. Not one word had been spoken.

83

Rachel and Vijay entered Chuck's office. Chuck got down to the issue right away, pointing to the picture in the newspaper before him. It showed Pjotr, elegantly dressed and in handcuffs, below the heading: *Head of Russian Cyber Mafia Arrested.*

This news triggered lead stories around the world. Not Pjotr per se had caused them, but the irresistible manner in which the news was published: the blogs of dozens of leading TV stations and newspapers were hacked and information placed on them – anonymously and for everyone to see. Chuck was thrilled:

„How clever this is. Kudos! That's publishing to my liking: not hampered by frontiers or censorship and appearing with a big bang."

They agreed, the noise the press was making had only just started and would turn into a storm, because the blog was huge. Most of its hundreds of files were still not translated let alone analyzed. But this would happen quickly, because the material was hot.

They scanned the part of the blog which was already translated automatically – emails, photos, names and addresses, records and dossiers. They tried to put the mess in order, sorting it according to media type, date or topic but soon gave up. It was too much.

Rachel: „Wow, someone did a good job tapping into press, banks, agencies and the mafia."

Chuck: „One guy told me the bog holds tons of news NSA knows nothing about which is a shock to them. Utterly inexplicable. So, NSA installed a task force: fifteen specialists are working on the blog and they will be busy for months. My source says they already found one hot trace in the Middle East."

Pacified, Chuck finally voiced what bugged him.

„My friends, I wish we had produced the blog. It would have been our victory."

He had no idea what had happened. Someone, Chuck guessed, must have been furious at Pjotr Denisowich, some insider or a rivaling gang. Or the government had blown him up.

The enormous variety of the blog's contents baffled them. The documents were old and new, some superficial others highly analytical and comprehensive. This ruled out the Russian Secret Services. They were not able to achieve what NSA could not. Rivals, too, could never have compiled the sheer volume of information. The Chinese or the Israelis might be capable of it. Perhaps they tested the latest technology in the field. But to post their results in public? This was out of the question.

Vijay looked at Rachel and smiled.

„One option remains: Eugen and his bot. No one else could have done it."

This remark struck Chuck like thunder:

„What? Did you say a bot? A bot could have done it?"

„Chuck, there is no other possibility."

Rachel: „I am beginning to believe in miracles. What a pity Bill isn't here. He'd cheer."

Chuck: „I am excited, too. My dream came true. Oh happy day. Come on, let's have lunch. You are invited, of course."

Rachel und Vijay found Chuck elated as never before:

„Let's have cocktails."

They started with a *Rusty Nail* and closed having a *Wall Banger*, but cocktails didn't help explain the mystery. Bill had stayed in touch with Eugen told him about the Wacko-affair and warned him. But Eugen never mentioned bots nor that he had progressed. And now a capital achievement, a breakthrough even? They decided, Bill should visit Eugen at once and see for himself. Then they would confer again.

84

Bill jumped up when Eugen arrived on the hill panting, and laid his bicycle on the ground.

„Gimme five, man."

They clapped hands and hugged.

„You are looking good, even got rosy cheeks. Your Porsche here keeps you fit."

„It was you who sent me here. Remember? It was the best you could do. Now you have one wish granted. How about holidays on a farm? Stay with us."

„Accepted. I promise. But not this time."

Bill pointed down to the abbey:

„Here it began. You spoke of a grand idea. I still can hear the echo of your words in the crypt."

„Hm. I bit off more than I could chew."

„How can you say that? Don't you read the papers? Look here! I bought them at the airport."

Bill opened his bag and pulled a pack of newspapers from all corners of the world, spreading them on the ground. All of them told the story of a Russian criminal hunted down in a most stupefying manner.

„Congratulations, my friend. You will win the Tour de France. You are already wearing the yellow jersey."

„Bah Humbug. None of us will ever be as famous as Pjotr. Only crooks and politicians make headlines."

„It is breaking my heart: no one knows your name and face. You will never win the Turing Prize like that."

„Nonsense. Just keep your fingers crossed that they won't get us, the vultures of the press."

„That's what I am doing. The press gives me the heebie-jeebies too. We are still working to keep the deluge under cover. It's a fulltime job for Chuck and me. That's why I must fly back tonight.

You are not out for fame and glory. That's good – it's saving you a lot of hassle. You only want perfection."

„I dreamed of perfection down in the crypt. And it's not over yet. I am still dreaming of the perfect theory – elegant and practical as well."

„You risked a lot for it."

„True. I gambled and risked everything. But I have not won, Bill."

„I don't get you. Your blog proves you reached your goal superbly. What more do you want?"

Reaching into his pocket Eugen produced a little object, then turned the palm of his hand up, placed a memory stick on it letting its golden casing sparkle in the sun.

„Here. The bot. Take it, it's for you."

Bill took the present with respect, felt it and read the engraving: *Anna*.

„The Golden Bot – the perfect creature from the hand of its creator. What a present."

„You are mistaken, I am not its creator. I don't even understand it, though I wished I would."

Bill stared at Eugen in disbelieve. He of all people should not understand and his bot at that. Should the rumors hold that he became a little odd, was still not entirely cured? Eugen smiled when he looked at Bill, noting his doubts.

„It sounds meshugga, I know. And yet it is true: I don't understand this creature. One distant day, perhaps, I will. If we then meet again, I can tell you a wondrous story of a unique creature which cured itself."

After the friends sat for a moment enjoying the company, Eugen fetched a bundle from his backpack, spread a tablecloth and served wine, cheese and bread.

„You see the hill over there? It's where Jean lured me with a picnic. And he hooked me."

They lifted the glasses and toasted. Soon after they parted. Bill hurried back in a car and Eugen rolled down the hill on his bike.

Eugen labored up the next hill, went along Henri's fields and turned into the farm. There Henri was sitting on a bench framed by a wisteria's blue blossoms.

„I am waiting for you. Anna said you will come. Day before yesterday it rained and yesterday it was warm. Now I go for mushrooms – I can smell them already. Come along and help. If you want to stay here, you must know the mushrooms. C'est normal. That's how it is."

They drove over into the Forêt de Lente, a forest covering several hilltops, where the time for boletus had come.

„Watch out for the cliff over there. And watch me looking for mushrooms. The weeds are too high here, they take all light away. Cèpes don't grow in the dark. And it's too swampy over there. They don't like wet feet either. Sometimes you must lie down on your belly and crawl into the brush. Look at me now."

They found many kinds of mushroom Eugen had never seen before, some soft and white with a blueish hue, another big as a soccer ball.

„Keep the cèpes. Slice and dry them or put them in oil. Fry the rest in butter and garlic. It's easy. And come over tonight and watch Marie-Thérèse cook a mushroom stew. It's great art."

Eugen returned to Sankt Petersburg, which he had left in a hurry. He intended to observe the upcoming trial of Pjotr Denisowich since he mistrusted the Russian justice system. And he wanted to meet Feiwel, his companion of old.

Feiwel had looked after Eugen's apartment and was promptly visited by Pjotr's men hunting for Eugen and threatening him. But he made them believe that Eugen planned to take off for good. Else he had not returned all computers to pay back his debt. He would bet ten bottles of vodka that Eugen moved south. Once he had raved about Uzbekistan, loony as he was.

It worked well for Eugen – his name didn't go on file in Pjotr's case – and he had time to spend with Feiwel who wanted to know about the adventures in the US and why he took root in the Drôme. While Eugen told his story, they were emptying the first bottle of cognac, Eugen's presents from France. Feiwel could not believe the strange things he heard of: an old tractor, paradise in a garden, cheese and mushrooms, old philosophy and the assumption that a bot found Phi, the number of life.

Eugen seemed strangely altered. Was this still the man he admired – once the engine and mastermind of an elite institute? It seemed, the former comrade director strayed from science.

„You are looking skeptical, my friend. Yes, what I am doing now I would not have done before. I am trying new things – in fact I am getting a kick out of it.“

„I get my kicks from the Denisovich-trial. It's juicy. Ha. First his love temple *The 5th Element* was closed. Next, the names of the clients were made public and nobody knows who found them out. Then they interviewed the girls. Wow. They not only loved the clients but also loved to talk about them. Believe me all of Russia had fun.

But it's not over yet. Aleksander was a regular, too, and you know whom I mean – the Great Councillor. He treated all his African and Latin American friends to a few happy hours. Then their names and photos leaked on the Internet. That turned into a diplomatic delicacy which beats all other news.

You have nothing to fear, Eugen. So, stay here and let's have fun together."

Eugen shook his head.

„No. I will go back. My game isn't over yet. And I hope a little time remains for me.

By the way, I like France and you would like it as I do. Come and see me. But come in spring when the morels grow. They are worth a trip, they say."

87

Chuck and Bill had Texan Chili con Carne for lunch while sharing news. Chuck learned about Bill's trip to Eugen and Bill about Chuck's meeting with Terry Hancock. Terry had followed the deluge with considerable concern and called in Chuck as soon as the blog appeared. Then he asked one question, Bill could not answer: *Has the project gone down the drain or can we save it?*

Now the golden casing of bot Anna lay on the kitchen table, gleaming, while Bill and Chuck went for a walk. Not the colors of the Indian summer lured them out of the house, but the need of fresh air to clear their minds, since the project had reached a turning point.

Chuck. „Now it's *Go* or *No Go*. After the meeting in Venice Beach you said the bot was dead. Now it is happy as never before and a copy is here right before us. Can we use it?

„Chuck you know the whole story. You know it as well as I do: even Eugen threw in the towel, doubting he would ever understand a bot which wasn't his creation at all. Who the hell knows what he means. I, for my part, don't."

Chuck nodded taking a deep breath. Then he clapped his notebook shut and slammed his palm on the table.

„It's decided now. We leave the bot in its golden cage and save it in a strongbox.

That's it, buddy. From now on you are going to enjoy more peace and quiet. Bill, I thank you a lot. What a grand job you did."

When Chuck was ready to part, Bill leaned to the open window of the car.

„A spark of hope remains. Eugen won't give up. Never. I felt his pride in the Golden Bot. He talked of it like of a daughter who outgrew him. He will care for her as long as he lives.

So, we got to wait and hope. Farewell, my friend, and have a safe trip."

88

There was a small issue Bill had kept quiet about. He led Chuck to believe he owned the only bot, the Golden Bot.

After the meeting with Eugen, Bill thought long and hard about what was to be done. He often hiked to Susan's Vista, came back to the garden, put the chairs before the rock and imagined Susan sitting beside him, offering her advice. So, he went through all the options he could think of and, at last, decided.

With Chuck's consent he would formally close the project and it would relieve him. He would meet Chuck one last time, possibly here in his home, after he had taken care of the team.

He considered passing copies of Eugen's bot on to each member of the team, hoping in secret that one day bots of a new generation would save America and settle what he deemed his personal disgrace: His country had called him and he did not help, did not prevent the project from running into the ground.

But he dismissed the idea. Rachel, Vijay and Joe would not change the situation. To give them the bot was not only useless, it was dangerous: bots could get lost, be misused or escape. Caution! Bots reminded him of a controversial issue: how to protect nuclear weapons in times of peace after the Cold War.

Finally, he thought of Betty's last words in Venice: *Hey, I will break Gödel's Curse or I'll die.* He never forgot these words. They seemed to resound as he pictured her – the graceful, silver-haired and iron-willed lady.

Then he called Betty and hearing her smitten voice, he knew she still had not made peace with bots. So, he invited her and she accepted with pleasure.

As they were sitting at the rock, Bill told her about the blog, the trip to Eugen and the Golden Bot. This blew her mind:

„This is impossible. It is ridiculous. Give me a break."

Bitter memories assailed her. Bill saw it while pulling a memory stick from his pocket:

„It is possible. Here is the bot, Eugen's gift."

„Then it must have escaped Gödel's curse. How can this be?"

„Nobody knows, not even Eugen. *I don't understand it,* he said."

All of a sudden, Betty was electrified. She grabbed Bill's hand, taking the memory stick.

„Let me do it. Give it to me. Please."

Bill had foreseen it. Betty would love this task, the meaning of her life.

Betty: „I don't believe I will succeed. Complexity will teach me another lesson – it is my cruel teacher. And yet there is hope – a tiny spark of hope. That's wonderful."

„The stick is for you, for you alone."

„Thanks Bill for thinking of me. Now, I will struggle and have fun, and perhaps even catch a glimpse of paradise."

After Betty returned to Venice Beach, Bill sat on the rock again, musing about his projects. Once he had had the job to watch the world via satellite, another time via bots. How odd. One team he had led to victory, the other to defeat. This defeat was hard to take but

Betty had helped him. She smiled as she said that being defeated by complexity was a honorable defeat. She even smiled as she spoke of her *death* and the hopes she had until then.

Bill thought of his own last hope. His ashes should find their way to Susan. Then grass and dandelions should grow on them.

89

„I tasted the grapes, Anna, they are ripe and sweet.“

„Yes, they are. Soon I will mix them with the cassis jelly. And you must not help me or spy. Look at the potatoes in the basket. Tonight we will have them au gratin. There you can help. It's no secret. Ha.“

Anna and Eugen were sitting on the garden bench, Eugen reporting of St. Petersburg, the meeting with Bill and that the project had come to an end.

„That's good. You will have more spare time. The ladies in my seminar asked for you by the way. They are so curious whether you managed to compute beauty and are happy about it. I guess you could entertain them splendidly.“

„We could talk about the *mysteries of bots* if they like. In the old bar.“

„And then they will embrace you. I know them. And Amelie will kiss you again.“

Anna now listened how Eugen letting his mind wander back to the unforgotten day Anna prepared for him – a composition of the four movements *Seminar, Bar, Gorge and Pass*. This day didn't illuminate him, but altered him. Somehow.

Anna: „I remember well. Then you wanted to find out about beauty. Now you want to know why a bot looks for beauty.

This question plagued Eugen a lot indeed. At night he sat before the workstation to find an answer – only to admit at last he had been chasing a mirage.

He had begun to doubt his abilities. At Stanford he always had at least a suspicion, why the bot failed. Thus, he had an idea which pushed him on and gave him hope. Now it seemed his reservoir of ideas had dried up.

He played with the thought of visiting Betty, a most capable person. But in the end, he knew, she could help as much as the ladies in Anna's seminar.

90

Anna witnessed how Eugen still exhausted himself and she pitied him.

„Did you ever consider why a human would look for beauty, someone who – like your bot – doesn't even know that beauty exists, thus someone who never went to school but walks the world with open eyes."

„Why should I? I am no psychologist. And bots have no soul."

Eugen heard himself talk and paused. What he said was not in order. Months ago he would have dismissed her idea as a woman's metaphysics. But now her question brought him back to his senses. *Anna never asked a stupid question – so listen and think, you blockhead*, he said to himself.

„Anna, what do you mean?"

„Well, I guess beauty attracts some people all the time and in all places. They recognize beauty in art and nature and wherever they see it. It seems natural like your love of Bach's music.

Other people recognize chaos. They sense it in themselves, when their thoughts and desires go haywire. Then they feel programmed with flaws. And they are afraid and often terrified of it.

These people seek a cure. They resort to beauty and perfection. Sometimes they flee to the healing womb called *order*."

Eugen sat silently. His eyes closed, he memorized what he had heard. Of chaos and fear Anna spoke, of flight and cure. These concepts would never have entered his mind.

He sighed and looked at Anna who quietly sat beside him. Thoughts swirled in his head. *Programmed with flaws,* she said. These word triggered memories. Again he saw the gloomy sight of his bot when the sensors proved the deadlock of its brain. It must have been the very moment when he lost control.

Now dark memories once more flooded his mind. He hated them and longed to run away, search mushrooms, peel potatoes, play Bach.

Anna felt him tremble. She moved closer, putting an arm around him.

„Anna, I love your touch. It's magic. It washed away my black thoughts in an instant."

People sense chaos inside, Anna had said, *therefore they often resort to order.* Now what about bots? What would they sense and to where would they resort? Slowly he formed an idea: Could it be that chaos raged in his bot.

That she knew something was wrong with her? That she couldn't trust her own brain?

Could it be that she looked for cure and found it in beauty?

„Anna, let's go and cook. I feel like it."

„O.k. then. We'll have ratatouille for supper. Today is your turn to do the chopping."

91

„Anna, a bot which heals itself – I cannot think of anything more absurd. It means I created a cripple and set her free. Please don't talk to anybody about this shame of mine. Not a word that I failed."

Anna smiled as she placed her cassis-cum-grape-creation on the table, offering a bit to Eugen.

„Taste it and try something new."

With a heavenly flavor on his tongue, Eugen returned Anna's smile.

Anna: „*Absurd* you said and *shame* and *cripple*, too. Nonsense, my friend. Just look at it from another point of view."

„Well?"

„You let your bot develop the way she wanted. And develop she did. Isn't it great?"

Eugen, who had never seen it this way, pondered.

Anna: „She achieved what you could not and became a good girl, too. Eugen, this is a gift."

„A gift?"

„You remember the evening we were talking at the fireplace?"

„Of course I do. Then I learned the words *kalós kai agathós* and still feel their rhythm."

„Then you said: *My bots are free*, and you were mighty proud of them. True, your bots enjoyed freedom, but you paid dearly for it. Perhaps you went too far."

Eugen nodded thinking of Betty's warning *Evolution is not a free lunch* and also of Rachel's accusation on the ranch: *You want to be god himself. It's a sin.* He groaned.

Anna: „Yes, you paid dearly, but you also won – think of your gift."

Eugen remembered the afternoon in the garden, when his bot's messages from Russia were pouring in. Then he sensed the unmatched feeling of pride and grace: his bot had overcome the last hurdle. Then he felt so very blessed: his bot, for the first time, worked the way she should. It was a gift indeed.

92

They were still sitting together in the early hours of the day, discussing *freedom* & *complexity*, *chance* & *necessity*, the *good* & *the beautiful* – what really mattered for bots.

Finally they touched on the concept of *beauty* – a bot's concept and not a human's concept. They still knew nothing about it and decided to study it: What does it look like, how is it used and what can it do?

Anna: „I hope we found the right question after all the toil and defeat."

„And when we have found the answer at last we will write it down: *The Story of Bot Anna.* Bill is waiting for it."

93

Meanwhile Betty was reactivating her testing gear of old. She had abandoned it decades ago, together with her dreams of next-generation knowledge systems. Her ideas of testing man-made intelligence, she knew, had not aged a bit and were still unmatched. And now they were red hot: no other technology could uncover what was happening inside the brain of a bot nearly as well.

She was so busy that Joe complained she was neglecting him. Indeed she hadn't accompanied him to the beach in a long time. She was hammering away on her keyboard, months of work ahead. Only when the testing suite ran on her workstation, would she witness why the old bot went down in the Bermuda Triangle and why the new bot survived it. Then at last would she understand bots and enter heaven.

∗∗∗

Abbey Saint Antoine